Dirk knew this shot
could be his last.

*

He raised on one knee, steadied the Colt
on the center of Shaver's mass and began
to squeeze the trigger.

"That will be enough."

This new voice came from his right
rear.

"Just like Shaver to mess it up. Give
him one for his own self and he can't even
do it right."

Dirk turned, knowing it was too late,
turned and brought the Colt around to this
new threat. Too late.

Too late.

He saw the barrel of a Colt, saw for
part of a second the beginning of a flash
of light as the hammer dropped.

Then his whole head seemed to explode
in white light and there was nothing.

Also by Paul Garrisen

DIRK'S REVENGE

**Coming soon from
HARPER PAPERBACKS**

PAUL GARRISEN

DIRK'S RUN

Harper Paperbacks

Harper & Row, Publishers, New York
Grand Rapids, Philadelphia, St. Louis, San Francisco
London, Singapore, Sydney, Tokyo, Toronto

This is a work of fiction. The characters, incidents, and dialogues are products of the author's imagination and are not to be construed as real. Any resemblance to actual events or persons, living or dead, is entirely coincidental.

Harper Paperbacks a division of Harper & Row, Publishers, Inc.
10 East 53rd Street, New York, N.Y. 10022

Cover art by George Bush

First printing: March, 1990

Printed in the United States of America

HARPER PAPERBACKS and colophon are trademarks of Harper & Row, Publishers, Inc.

10 9 8 7 6 5 4 3 2 1

DIRK'S RUN

C·H·A·P·T·E·R

☆ ——————— *1* ——————— ☆

DUNCAN—"Dirk"—Prine dismounted
stiffly. He was twenty-eight and had only
ridden ten miles since breaking camp
and wouldn't normally have been stiff. But his leg
wound—a .44 ball in his upper thigh at Bull Run
before they cashiered him out of the army—still
acted up when the weather was changing though
it had been four years and more since the rebel
captain had popped the cap on him.

Tracks went out in front of him and he wondered how long he'd been watching them without
really knowing it.

Three, no, four horses. All shod with deep-
cleated dirt shoes. Not too fresh. Maybe a day,
maybe a bit more. Riding the same way Dirk was

moving. Four men or two men, he wasn't that good at tracking.

West.

He removed his hat and used his index finger to wipe the sweat band clean, then flicked the sweat away and put the hat back on his head.

It was hot and he'd come four hours since water. He was riding a big bay named Hammer and like most big horses he needed water almost constantly.

Dirk tied the bay off to a limb on some willows next to the trail and took the one-gallon wool-covered canteen from the saddle. He'd been careful with it but it was still half gone. The bay had taken most of it.

"I ought to have a barrel with me," he muttered to the bay while he held the horse's head up and poured water in the side of his mouth. The bay drank expertly until Dirk pulled the canteen away. The bay's head followed it, trying to suck more water, and Dirk slapped him on the nose gently. "Not likely. . . ."

He took a small sip for himself and put the canteen back on the horn, still thirsty.

"Thing is," he said, looking west at the start of some low rolling hills, "I don't have any idea where we're going—or how far it is to water."

Dirk had been riding west, letting the bay pick his way, for close to two weeks since leaving Little Rock.

Not looking for anything, not looking to get anywhere, he'd been moving that way since the war ended and he'd healed from the wound. At least the one that showed. Some of the other ones, the deep ones, didn't heal so fast.

He'd listened to the drums, listened to the pretty speeches and seen the waving flags and pennants, and had enlisted.

It was his last innocent act.

He'd joined in Pennsylvania with the 63rd just in time for Gettysburg. He swung into the saddle and let the bay start moving again.

Gut-scared—that was all he remembered of it now. Being gut-scared at the lines of men who came on and on, firing at him in clouds of smoke and whistling minié balls.

Slaughter. Endless slaughter and he could not believe he hadn't been hit. Men on both sides had gone down, cut and been blown down, and somehow Dirk had been missed.

And every battle after that. He'd had both heels shot off his boots, a kepi shredded on his head, a musket blown out of his hands, and never hit until some rebel captain had looked at him, aimed, and put the ball in his hip.

The bay followed the tracks of the four horses and Dirk let him move on at his own speed.

"Maybe they know where there's water," he said aloud.

He rode well. He was set up solidly, stood five

eleven, and had tight muscles so that his movements helped the horse, and he spent the rest of
the afternoon riding easily.

It was low break country. Coming out of the
rough gullies and ridges of Arkansas into the
muggy heat of eastern Oklahoma the land broke
into almost gentle hills.

Dirk had been watching the tracks more
closely—again without meaning to—and he saw
where one of the horses had hit some damp sand
near the trail. The hoofprints were still partially
dark in the low places.

"Less than a day."

He did not want to run up on the men and he
did not know why. Part of it was how his thinking
worked. He'd been riding alone for so long now
he didn't want company, but it was more than
that. Something about the tracks bothered him.

Why four men?

The war was done. Men riding home would be
long home.

A man riding, two men—but four was too
many. There were bands of men left from the war,
scavengers who could not stop thinking war. Hard
men.

"Ahh hell." He shook his head. "I'm getting
skitchy about nothing. See a few tracks . . ."

He stood in the stirrups and stretched in the
saddle. It was close to evening and he decided to
make a dry camp.

He dismounted, untied his bedroll, and tied the bay off on a long line so it could graze on what sparse grass there was.

Dirk worked with practiced ease. He could not really remember when he hadn't slept outside. Even on the farm back in Pennsylvania—two, three hundred years ago, he thought, smiling tightly—even there he spent most of his time outside, slept in the barn when he wasn't sleeping in the hills. His dad worked on a jug all the time and it made him mean so Dirk simply stayed away and when he was fourteen he never went back again.

In what seemed like moments, he had the camp set up, his bedroll laid out under a slicker—though it didn't look like rain—firewood gathered, a fire going, and a pot of beans and salt pork he'd bought from an Arkansas farmer brewing next to a pan with coffee grounds and hot water.

He took his gun belt off and laid the Colt on the bedroll, then sat down next to it and leaned back against the saddle that he'd put at the head of his roll underneath the wool blanket.

Home, he thought, and wondered why he hadn't gotten sick of it. Even the army hadn't soured him on being outside. It soured him on sleeping with two or three hundred farting, shitting, snoring, and snorting men—he liked to be alone before the army and more so now. But he still liked being out in it, the weather.

The water in the pan with the coffee boiled and he reached to pull it out of the flames.

"Keep that hand out, or I'll blow a hole up your ass you could park a wagon in."

The voice came from over his right shoulder. Dirk kept his hand out but turned his head slightly and could see a man in the willows. He couldn't tell much about the man in the bad light except that he was dirty with trail dust.

And he was holding a sawed-off double-barrel Greener twelve-gauge aimed at Dirk.

C·H·A·P·T·E·R

☆ ——— 2 ——— ☆

"CARLEY said I should double back. He said it and he was right." The man with the shotgun wobbled his head while he spoke, like a turkey, but the barrels on the Greener didn't move. "He said, Shaver, you work back careful and quiet like and you'll see some son of a bitch that's been following us for nigh on two days. You find him and you can kill him. . . ."

Dirk tried to see beyond the man in the dark. He had almost no chance against the Greener, but if the man was alone, at least there would be only the one gun. If he had friends coming up, Dirk was probably dead. Probably was anyway. His Colt was maybe eight inches from his hand—

might as well be a mile. Maybe he could talk around it.

"I wasn't following you," Dirk said. "I was just riding. . . ."

"It don't matter. Carley said I get to kill you and I get to kill you. You got a watch?" He smiled, not unkindly. "I'd like it if you'd give me the watch before I shoot you. This damn scattergun makes such a mess and if it gets into the watch. . . ."

"I don't have a watch." Dirk moved his hand, almost imperceptibly, toward the Colt.

"How about paper money? You get blood and guts mixed in with paper money and even a Cherokee Strip whore won't take it."

Dirk nodded. A chance. If he could move and lean at the same time, just a small lean. "I've got some in my pants pocket. I'll have to move to get at it."

"Go ahead—slow."

Dirk leaned over to his right, which brought his hand closer to the Colt.

He saw it all in his mind's eye—what he had to do. Fall over to the right, grab the Colt, slam the hammer back, and fire—and hit the bastard— all in less time than he could swing the barrel on the Greener a few inches and pull the trigger.

Not a chance.

But it's all I have, he thought, and made his move.

It almost went as he planned. As he fell side-ways he heard one barrel of the shotgun roar and felt a nudge on the side of his upper arm where the charge scraped him.

At the same time he got his hands on the Colt, slapped the hammer back, and fired through the bottom of the holster.

Unfortunately the blow of the shot taking his upper arm swung him around so that the bullet from the Colt went nowhere near where it was supposed to go—namely into any part of Shaver.

Instead the big slug hit almost dead center in the pan filled with boiling water and coffee.

The hydraulic shock of the .45 long Colt bullet turned the hot coffee into an exploding bomb and a great deal of the scalding water found its way into Shaver's face before he could pull the trigger on the Greener's second barrel—which was aimed exactly at the middle of Dirk's chest.

Shaver screamed, dropped the shotgun, and went over backward clawing at his face.

Dirk jerked the Colt free of the holster, thumbed the hammer back, and fired again, then once more as he rolled across the bedroll and out into the dirt away from the fire.

He thought he hit meat on the third shot but couldn't be sure. Shaver was screaming and roll-ing around on the ground.

Another one, he thought—memory from the

war—if they're still moving get another one in them.

He raised himself on one knee, steadied the Colt on the center of Shaver's mass, and began to squeeze the trigger.

"That will be enough."

This new voice came from his right rear.

"Just like Shaver to mess it up. Give him one for his ownself and he can't even do it right."

Dirk turned, knowing it was too late, turned and brought the Colt around to this new threat. Too late.

Too late.

He saw the barrel of a Colt, saw for part of a second the beginning of a flash of light as the hammer dropped.

Then his whole head seemed to explode in white light and there was nothing.

C·H·A·P·T·E·R

☆ ——— 3 ——— ☆

"**I**T'S the pizen, goddammit!" The voice was muffled, came in thuds like a drum in water. "You're such a dumb shit you don't even know about pizen?"

Dirk knew, remembered nothing. Just the voice, coming from far away, miles away.

"Well, shit, the bullet took him in the head—you ain't gonna get nuffin' out of his goddamn belly."

"Chest," the first voice cracked. "You damn rummy—the pizen centers in the chest and down the guts from there. That's why you tar the chest and belly with the poultice. *That's* where you get the pizen out."

Dirk opened his eyes—or tried to. There was something over them, tied tight around his head, and when he tried to move his head, or even when he tried to move his eyelids to free them, the pain came.

The pain was not tolerable, not understandable—it was as if a gun suddenly went off *inside* his brain; a volcano in his head.

"Unnnnnh." The sound seemed to come from someone else.

"See, Pisspot, the poultice is working already—he's coming around."

But I'm not, Dirk thought, or thought he thought—I'm dying.

And he slipped under again, spiraling down through the pain until he was gone.

The next time Dirk awakened, or came to, there was bright light slashing into his eyes. Again the pain blasted him and again he tried to open his eyes—only this time he didn't pass out and his eyelids came up.

To see nothing.

At first he was confused, thought he must be blind, but in a moment he realized there was something tied over his eyes, wrapped around his head.

With this knowledge suddenly came other awareness.

He could hear. There were at first no voices, but he heard birds singing and a *whuff*ing sound that he realized was a dog panting nearby.

Pain came and went in waves and he had to lay back for a moment until it passed again.

As soon as he controlled it he opened his eyes again and tried to move his arms and was surprised to find that both of his arms and legs were tied off.

He was apparently stretched flat on his back on some kind of bed on a platform, his arms tied above his head and his ankles tied off below and out to either side.

He heard flies now, buzzing the wrapping on his head, and he remembered the wound.

Hell, he thought, I can't be alive—that bastard shot me full on in the face. I saw the flash.

Dirk opened his eyes once more. The wrapping was loosened a bit and by moving his head carefully, slowly to the side—the pain was riveting—he at last got one eye free.

Light bored into the eye and he blinked, squinted, and looked at his surroundings.

He was looking at the ceiling in an old shack. The walls, the ceiling—the whole building was falling apart. He could see sunlight through the roof and outside through the walls. Old clothing hung on nails, almost unbelievably dirty, and with his vision blurry, somehow his smell was triggered.

The odor was staggering. Somewhere between rotting meat—a smell he remembered well from battles—and ancient dust.

The whuffing dog that had been in a corner stood and walked toward him. It was an old hound so skinny Dirk thought he could see damn near through him.

The hound licked the wrapping on his head three or four times, then walked away, and as Dirk's eye followed him, he at last saw his body.

"Christ. . . ."

He was totally nude. Lashed on his back, tied down stark naked, and smeared all over his chest, down his stomach, and into his groin was a thick, black substance dried to the consistency of thick, hard glue.

He knew the substance, knew what it was, but he couldn't think of it.

"Well, shit, Pisspot, lookee here—he's awake. I told you the poultice would work."

Two old men came into the shack, into his vision. They were walking versions of the rags on the wall.

The one apparently named Pisspot leaned over him and used one finger to raise the bandage so Dirk could see out of both eyes.

Dirk frowned in a new squint, then stared at them. "Who are you?"

"I'm Pisspot Jimmy and this here other one who thinks he saved your ass is Mob."

"Yes, but . . ."

"Nothing to know about," Pisspot said. "We found you . . ."

"Like Moses in them bullroachers," Mob cut in. "Just a-laying there all nekked as the day you was borned. . . ."

"Yeah," Pisspot said. "Sort of—you was naked and somebody had shot you in the head. . . ."

"Scavengers," Dirk said. "They came up on me just at dusk."

Pisspot nodded. "We rode on you in the morning—must have been the next morning. We were following a mule that got away from us. . . ."

"It was a miracle!" Mob jumped around in a circle with his arms raised. "The mule led us to you just like Moses in them bullroachers and then I made my poultice and took out the pizen and you *lived*!"

"Yeah." Pisspot nodded. "Sort of. The man who shot you must have jerked his shot because the ball kind of went under the skin but slid along the head bone around the side. Made an ugly hole—we had to pick fly eggs out of her with a spoon—but saved your life. . . ."

Dirk took a shallow breath and felt whatever was on his chest and stomach pull at the hairs. "What's all over me?"

"That's my miracle poultice," Mob said, leaning forward over the bed and Dirk's face. His breath, Dirk thought, smelled like a swamp. "It took all the pizen out of you, see. All that pizen is in the poultice. . . ."

"What is the poultice made of?" Dirk asked.

His eyes were used to the light now and he decided they were both at least a hundred years old and that they were the dirtiest, ugliest men he'd ever seen.

"My magic poultice is made of pine tar and secret things passed on by the old Indians lo these many many years."

Pisspot held up his hand. "That's enough, Mob. You take on too damn much."

Dirk leaned his head back and closed his eyes, and at that precise moment Mob grabbed the slab of tar at the top edge of Dirk's chest and with a mighty heave tore it loose, along with all his stomach and chest hairs.

"Arrrnnnng!"

Dirk screamed and lunged against the ropes, which bumped his head against the end of the bunk, and his brain blew him into unconsciousness again.

He came back up at night. There was a chill, and when he opened his eyes in the full moonlight he could see that one of the old men had covered him with a scratchy, old blanket.

More, they had untied his arms and legs.

He ran his hands down his chest and stomach. I'm bald, he thought—there isn't a hair. And still naked.

He rolled on his side and eased his legs over the

side. Dizziness took him as he sat up, but he put his hand to the wall and it passed.

When it had settled completely, he stood—with one hand on the wall—and took two steps.

He didn't have a plan, wasn't thinking—just wanted to be on his feet.

In the corner the hound growled, but it wasn't menacing, just a sleep rumble.

On the other side of the shack he saw the two old men lying on the floor. There was a jug between them and they were passed out.

Clothes, Dirk thought. First clothes.

He felt along the wall in the old rags and coats and found an old pair of trousers. They were torn, filthy, and too big for him, but he put them on, leaning against the wall and swaying, and they made him feel better.

He felt farther along the wall and found a canvas jacket and put that on.

And now a gun, he thought, now a gun.

But he was tired and he felt his way silently back to the bunk and lay down to rest.

To sleep.

D IRK sat on the edge of the bunk eating beans and what Pisspot said was rabbit but which looked like ground squirrel. Pisspot and Mob sat on boxes eating out of old metal pie pans used as plates.

"How long have I been here?" Dirk asked around a mouthful of rabbit/squirrel. His head wound was closing nicely, though still tender. The food seemed to go right into his muscles, build them, fill them.

"I'm not sure," Pisspot said. The hound took a chance at Pisspot's plate and the old man hit him so hard the dog's slobber went all over the wall. "Must be going on two weeks. . . ."

" 'Twere exackly seventeen days since he come

to us like Moses in the bullroachers—he come to us like a babe, all naked and nurtured. . . ."

"He gets buggered up in his thinking," Pisspot said, "but his numbers are straight and he can ride a mule like he was painted to the son of a bitch."

Dirk finished the beans and put the plate on the floor for the hound to lick clean. He had learned that they would do it anyway.

"My head is healing," he said. "And I'm getting stronger. I'm going to have to leave. . . ."

"You *can't* leave," Mob said. "You come on us like a babe and now you belong to us. . . ."

Dirk ignored Mob. He had learned a bit about the two men in the past week. They were brothers and had lived on the edge of the Oklahoma Territory for close to twenty years, doing whatever they had to do to live.

"We robbed a stage oncet," Mob had told Dirk in a moment of lucidity. "Took sixteen dollars and eighteen cents off a drummer who sold fancy women's under pretties and all Pisspot had to do was shoot him a little in the foot. He had a catalog would tighten your stomach but Pisspot told me to quit looking at it before it made me commit 'bominations. . . ."

A few years before the war they had picked up some brood mares and two stud burros and ever since they had been raising and breaking mules that they sold once a year to the army over in Ft. Sill.

"Them soldier boys can ride 'em and pack 'em but they can't break 'em," Pisspot said to Dirk one afternoon. "Ain't that passing strange?"

As near as Dirk could figure it, Mob had been kicked in the head while breaking horses and mules at least half a dozen times.

"His brains are half scrambled," Pisspot explained. "And the other half was pounded out his ass a long time ago." He spit a stream of tobacco juice at the hound. "But his heart's good and he's sound as a dollar when you need him."

"Where in hell you going?" Pisspot said now, jerking Dirk's thoughts back to the present. "You ain't got but half a head your ownself and no horse nor clothes nor nothing. . . ."

Dirk nodded. "I know all that's true but I'm sound enough to ride and the truth is those sons of bitches have got a two-week start on me. . . ."

Pisspot stared at him. "You ain't really going after them, are you?"

"Oh, woe; oh, woe," Mob cried. "We saved baby Moses from the bullroaches and now he's going back into the lion's den."

The truth was until he said it Dirk didn't really know what he was going to do. But now that it was out in the open he knew it was the truth.

"Why you doing this?" Pisspot asked. His old face broke in a frown, creasing ancient dirt. "They like to killed you oncet, what makes you think you can best 'em now?"

For a moment Dirk said nothing. The truth was he wasn't sure if he could best the riders, or even find them—or what he would do if he *did* find them.

"That isn't it," he said. "It isn't, can I best them or not—I just can't let it ride."

Pisspot studied him but said nothing. Clearly it made no sense to the old man. Mob watched the flies moving over the hound in the corner as if they were the only thing in the world.

"They're going to kill you," Pisspot said evenly. "Kill you clean and down, if you do find them."

Dirk nodded. The old man was right. "Probably."

"Truth is me and Mob have come to be fond of you," Pisspot said. "We like having you around."

Dirk thought for a time on how to tell them a reason for what he was doing.

"It's the war," he said at length. "The goddamn war. We fought and fought and we killed each other for not one damn thing except that it shouldn't happen again. . . ."

"Oh, hell," Pisspot said. "Me and Mob fought down in that Messican war. That was the same. We fought to take Messico which we didn't keep and them Messicans fought to keep it and they didn't want it. It was all shit, just all shit. That don't mean me and Mob want to go off and get killed. . . ."

Dirk shook his head. "It isn't that—I'm not doing it to get killed. It was just that all of it, all that fighting—it didn't mean but one thing to me." He paused, looking out the window. "It meant that men like that wouldn't be able to do what they did and just ride. Not ever, not ever again—not to me."

Pisspot nodded. "That's the young in you. Hell, me and Mob were down in El Paso when we had the young on and I shot a man in the belly button just for spitting on my boot—but you learn when you get old that it don't amount to much, being young. Don't amount to nothing."

All the while that he was talking he was up, moving around the shack, rummaging in corners. Finally he grunted in satisfaction and pulled out an old, wooden dynamite box.

"Here it is. . . ."

On the side of the box was written:

HERCULES

60 PERCENT

It had a makeshift lid that was fastened with a rusty latch. Pisspot had stopped talking now as he worked at the latch to break the rust loose. It was stubborn and he found a hoof pick to use as a lever before it broke.

"There. I ain't been in this box for close on twenty years but I packed her in thick grease so she ought to be all right. . . ."

Mob had been sitting in the corner with the hound, but he now rose and came over to watch Pisspot dig in the dynamite box.

He brought out several bundles of rags thick with grease and oil. These he laid carefully on the bed, arranging them in separate piles.

Mob sat on the bunk next to the bundles and touched them tenderly.

Pisspot picked up one of the bundles and unwrapped the rags. Inside was a bullet mold, a bar of pig lead, and a brass powder flask with an eagle emblazoned on the side. In the spout of the flask was jammed a cork that had then been coated with wax.

He shook the flask and smiled when he heard the powder move loosely inside. "Still good. . . ."

The mold he laid carefully to the side with the bar of lead. Then he picked up the next bundle and unwrapped it.

"It's like Christmas," Mob said, smiling toothlessly.

The next bundle contained a holster and belt. It was a large military holster with a top flap on it, and the belt was black leather. The leather on both was dull but coated thickly with grease and still supple. It came to a shine when Pisspot rubbed it briskly with a rag before laying it aside.

Dirk leaned forward and turned the buckle in the light. It was heavy brass and showed an eagle holding a snake in its talons.

"Mob took it off a Messican," Pisspot explained. "He didn't need it anymore."

Dirk touched the leather on the holster and belt, thinking of the Mexican soldier. They were all the same, he thought, soldiers—the man who owned this belt did not think he would die.

Pisspot took out the last bundle, laid it on the bed, and unwrapped it almost with reverence. When it was open Dirk could see that it was a gun, a revolver, but not one he'd ever seen before, though he'd heard of them.

It was a Walker Colt Dragoon—a giant of a horse pistol that weighed over five pounds when loaded. At first it was hard to tell anything about the gun. It was coated fingernail deep in congealed axle grease. But Pisspot used a corner of the rag to clean some of the grease off, then dropped the loading lever and removed the huge cylinder with its long .44 caliber holes and put it down on the rag.

He held the pistol frame up and found a clean corner of the rag to get the rest of the grease off the steel, and when he did, it was clear the gun was in excellent shape.

"Twenty years?" Dirk said. "And it looks that good?"

"It's all in the grease. If you don't let air in she won't rust. I put her away when we came back from that Messican business—took it off a dead colonel, one of ours—and swore I'd never take her out again. I wanted to throw it away but Mob, he wouldn't let me."

It was evident that Mob loved the gun. His eyes were alight and he took the cylinder from the bed and used another piece of rag to clean it, wiping it over and over as he rolled it in his hand. "Borned again—come out with mess on it, just like a babe, born in the fire and raised in the fire for baby Moses to strike down the Phillippines. . . ."

Pisspot took the cylinder from his brother and slipped it back into the frame.

Dirk looked up sharply. "Me? The gun is for me?"

Pisspot nodded. "Mob is right. The gun is for you. . . ."

Dirk shook his head. "I couldn't. It's your gun. It wouldn't be right."

Pisspot studied him, his face tipped sideways as if pulled over by the weight of the tobacco in his cheek. He spit on the wall. "That ain't it. You just don't think it's much of a gun."

Dirk shook his head again, though there was some truth in what he said. "No. I've heard of them in the war—somebody said some officers were carrying them tied to their saddles, but I never saw any of them. They're all right for a cap-lock, but I got used to cartridges and my thumb-buster Colt. I'm not sure I could even shoot that old Dragoon.''

Pisspot sighed. ''There are none so blind as will not see. Truth is, boy, this Dragoon will put your Colt to shame. With dry powder and hot caps she'll put a bull down and hold tight doing it. The weight makes her steady. Let me load this and I'll show you.''

He unstoppered the powder flask and set it aside. Then he went to a cupboard and found a small box of caps. Six of these he put on the nipples on the Walker Colt cylinder and aiming the gun at the floor he fired all six of them.

''You have to burn the oil and grease out of the nipples or she'll misfire. . . .''

Dirk knew all this—he had carried cap and ball pistols in the war, although they were Remingtons, both smaller and less powerful than the Walker—but he said nothing.

Pisspot cleaned the broken copper pieces of cap out of the nipple holes, then rummaged again in the dynamite box and pulled out a small cracked leather sack full of lead balls.

He poured powder into a cylinder hole until it was nearly half an inch from the top—as much as would normally go in a rifle—and dropped a ball on the open end of the hole. It was too large for the opening and he rotated it beneath the loading lever and, grunting, levered the ball down into the hole. Because of its larger size it shaved a healthy ring of soft lead from the ball as he pushed it down until it was jammed on top of the powder and just even with the end of the cylinder. This ring of lead he flicked away with his fingernail.

"The more lead you cut off," he said, loading the next hole, and the next, "the righter she'll group. Cutting the sides this way turns them into bullets and they take the rifling better."

That Dirk hadn't known, but again, he chose to say nothing. Mob watched all of it, the loading, the speaking, as if watching a minister or priest perform a religious ritual. Flies landed on his face and he didn't brush them away; the gun, every part of it, held him completely.

When all the chambers in the cylinder were loaded, Pisspot took the gun to a small bucket of lard in the corner. He dabbed a healthy chunk of the fat on the end of his finger and worked it down on top of each ball, pushing the grease hard, and when all the balls were covered with lard he wiped his hand on his pants and put six caps on the nipples.

"You don't lard them like that, squeeze it down hard on each ball, and the fire will jump from one cylinder to the next when you fire. Saw a boy

break his wrist when he did that once in a hurry—
the gun bucked back so hard.''

He squeezed each small copper cap to pinch it
slightly together before putting it on.

''Otherwise, they're loose and the gun jump
might knock them off. . . .''

He set the hammer on a safety notch between
two nipples and left the shack. The three men
went out in back of the building where a dry
streambed cut through some willows.

Mob had followed along quietly, walking
slightly in back of Dirk, but when they got to the
streambed he moved forward and stood loosely
next to Pisspot, still silent.

Dirk was surprised to see Pisspot hand Mob the
Walker.

''I don't shoot, myself,'' Pisspot said. ''Not
since that Messican business.'' He looked sharply
at Dirk, waiting for a reaction, but Dirk remained
quiet; he knew many men after the war who
would not shoot. Not even to hunt.

''Besides, with Mob here I don't have to shoot.
Mob, the aspen over there three times.''

He said it all in one breath, without breaking
between the words, but before the sentence was
out Mob shrugged his shoulders, strength filled
his old body, seemed to flow from the gun into
him and fill him, raise him.

Then his arm tightened, the Walker came up
and bellowed three times. It was unnaturally loud

and impossibly fast—the shots so close together they sounded like one long explosion—and the streambed was immediately filled with a huge cloud of gray smoke as the black powder blew out of the massive gun.

It was impossible to see across the streambed, but before the smoke had obscured his vision Dirk had seen something he wasn't sure he believed.

Across the streambed an aspen about three inches in diameter broke at the base and went over—seemed to jump from itself—as one of the balls took out a large chunk of wood. For a handgun to pack that much—to take the small tree off—was hard enough to believe. But before the smoke filled the streambed he saw the aspen start to fall and as it went down it was hit twice more, once two feet above the original shot and again two feet above that; hit while it was moving, falling, clean in the middle and broken twice more.

Dirk turned to stare at Mob but the old man ignored him. He stood with his shoulders slouched, the Walker hanging at his side.

"It was ever like this," Pisspot said. "Even as a boy before he took to getting kicked in the head it was ever like this. Hand him a gun and he couldn't miss. Used to shoot birds flying with the squirrel rifle back in Pennsylvania and it got so they wouldn't let him shoot at the turkey shoots no more 'cause he just took everything."

Pisspot took the gun from Mob and handed it to Dirk. "Take a shot. Hold her with both hands but don't put nothing ahead of the cylinder. She blows sideways something fierce."

Dirk took the Walker and was surprised at how heavy it proved to be. Hog, he thought—hog steel. Hell, it's got a hammer weighs more than my whole Colt. But then—he smiled grimly—I don't have a Colt anymore, do I?

He toggled the hammer, held it with both hands, aimed at a rock across the streambed, and squeezed.

The Walker roared with another cloud of smoke and kicked back up and right, almost tearing itself out of his hand. The dirt flew about four inches to the right of the rock.

"You're jerking her," Pisspot said, shaking his head. "Gotta squeeze her."

"Like holding a newborned babe fresh from the bullroachers," Mob cut in, "gotta just squeeze and squeeze. . . ."

Dirk looked at them. Sergeants had told him the same thing, corporals had told him the same thing, privates first class had told him the same thing, and none of it worked. He couldn't target shoot. But when it mattered where the ball went he got the job done. It rankled him to stand and take instructions like some kind of wet-eared recruit. "I went through the whole damn war," he said, "and I generally hit what I aimed at."

Pisspot nodded, unruffled. "Just trying to refine your abilities a bit, son. Go ahead, shoot the other two balls out."

Dirk did as he was told, holding carefully and squeezing—or "squeeeezing," as Mob told him again—but he didn't hit the rock, although on the last shot he got within three or four inches of it.

Pisspot shook his head. "Pretty bad, pretty bad—we'd better do her again."

He took the big Colt back to the shack, reloaded it, and made Dirk fire it six more times, and then another six, shaking his head ruefully with each shot before he at last sighed. "Well, I guess that's as good as you'll get—you can't make a hawk out of a Dominiker, can you?"

"Now wait a minute. . . ." Dirk started, his ears still ringing from the hammering the Walker had given them, but Pisspot ignored him.

"Got to think by way of sitting you now, don't we, Mob?" Pisspot scratched himself as he sat on the bunk and leaned back against the wall.

He had heated a pan of water on the small cookstove and was making Dirk use a rag and the hot water to clean the black powder residue from the Walker. Just shooting it eighteen times had left the smoke-dirt (as Pisspot called it) thick in each crack. The cylinder pin was so coated with it the cylinder itself only turned with difficulty and Dirk had to pour water down alongside the cylinder axis to get the pin out.

"What do you mean?" Dirk asked.

"Gotta seat you," Mob said. "Gotta send you out in the world. Found you like a babe in the bullroachers and now we got to send you out in the world to part the waters. . . ."

"We mean you've got to have a mount," Pisspot corrected. "We'll cut out a mule in the morning and Mob can green her out for you."

Dirk shook his head—realized he seemed to spend most of his time with these two shaking his head. "You can't be giving me all this. . . ."

"How did you figure on leaving?" Pisspot asked. "Was you gonna walk? Hell, be they headed west it's prob'ly twenty, twenty-five miles to the nearest ranch where you could find a mount. Then you'd have to steal it or work it off. You don't have diddly, not diddly to spend."

And of course he was dead right. "Well. I'll send money back when I can."

"No. You won't. We want to do this and we'll do this and there ain't one goddamn thing you can say about it."

"You're ours," Mob cried. "Our babe to send off into the world for to part the waters and make your way—our own babe."

Dirk looked at Mob and thought, Some mother. Some mothers I've got. Christ. But he nodded. "I thank you then. . . ."

"Now let's eat," Pisspot said, rubbing his hands. "Mob, he went out last night with the dog while we were sleeping and got a possum. It's been in the creek all day so's it would stay fresh, and we'll stew it up and have a big farewell supper."

"A last supper," Mob added. "It will be our last supper before we send our babe out in the world to make his own way." He went out to clean the possum while Pisspot took the same pan Dirk had been using to clean the Colt, threw the black, dirty water out through a crack in the wall, and added water from a bucket by the door—where Dirk had seen the hound drinking—and put it on the stove. He threw in a few pieces of dry pine and the fire kicked up in a moment.

Dirk studied Mob through the open doorway. He was down by the stream dropping the guts out of the possum, handing them to the hound who gratefully swallowed them before they hit the ground. Sometimes Mob didn't seem half as crazy as he did at other times. "How is it he came by the name—Mob?"

Pisspot paused, watching his brother down by the stream. Then he scratched himself and grunted.

"It was down in that Messican business. Come a day outside Chihuahua in some desert break country—God *damn* but it was dry down there. You couldn't even spit. I know men quit pissing for three, four days—just didn't have any water in them."

"Mob," Dirk prompted. "You were telling me about his name."

"Oh. Yeah. So come a day down in that desert break country and Mob somehow got separated. He was always one to go off looking at things, even when he was a pup. Drove our ma crazy sometimes. She was always worried he'd get in the pigs and get et. . . ."

"His name."

"All right, all right, I'm getting to it. So come a day down there when it was so dry you couldn't spit and Mob got off alone and I didn't get to thinking of him right away. So's it must have been two, three hours before anybody really noticed he was missing. We were bivvied in a canyon but it was along a range of bluffs where there was lots of other canyons."

He scratched and took a moment to spit through the wall. "So finally I got to missing him, couldn't find him. I got a few of the other men and we looked and still couldn't find him until finally one of them said they'd seen him take a mount and head off in the direction of one of the other canyons.

"Well, naturally we took some horses and hied off looking for him and we found him."

He paused, remembering how it had looked, then, quietly, he repeated it. "We found him. He was sitting on a rock holding up one of those little red flowers come on prickly pear cactus. He was looking at it and smelling it and holding it this way and that way and when I rode up to him he looked up at me and said, 'Have you ever seen anything so pretty?' "

He paused again, held it so long that Dirk prompted, "That's it? He just went to pick flowers?"

"No." Pisspot sighed. "I was just remembering how it looked. Him sitting on that rock, holding that flower, and all around him death. Death and destruction. He'd run into a patrol of Messican cavalry in the little canyon. He'd gone in there to look at flowers and he'd run into that patrol and he'd killed them all.

"Eight men lay dead around him in the dirt. And their horses. Dead. And Mob's horse, too. All dead. He'd killed them all, killed everything around him, and there he sat on that rock holding that little flower up to the light." Pisspot shook his head. "Damnedest thing I ever saw, ever."

He turned away to put potatoes in the pan on the stove and Dirk sat thinking of what he'd said; how Mob could have killed eight armed soldiers. It didn't seem possible—and yet after seeing him shoot at the streambed maybe it did. Then he remembered something. "Hey, wait a minute—you still didn't tell me how he got his name."

"Oh—one of the men with me, when we come up on him and saw all dead bodies, said, 'Lookee there, he's killed him a whole mob.' And the name stuck."

He dropped the potatoes in the pan and Mob came in then with the cleaned possum. He cut it in pieces and dropped them in the pot, then turned to Dirk.

"Babe from the roachers, plucked him clean and saved him, needs one more thing. . . ."

"A mount," Pisspot put in, then he looked down at Dirk's feet. "And a pair of good boots. Which we don't have." Dirk was wearing a pair of old brogan work shoes Pisspot had given him, with one floppy sole.

Mob nodded. "That and that and that and a hat. He's got no cover for his head and the sun will make him daft, make him into a Mob. . . ."

Above the entryway to the shack was a shelf made from a split log. Mob took another dynamite box from the shelf and set it gently on the bed.

Inside the box Dirk could see a feed sack containing an object with some bulk to it. Mob removed the feed sack and untied the end, reached inside as if reaching for eggs, and pulled out a surprisingly clean, perfectly formed and blocked derby.

"A hat for the babe," he said, handing the hat to Dirk. "For to keep his head from the sun. . . ."

Dirk took the hat. He knew not to argue now,

that Mob would not have offered it if he didn't want Dirk to have it, so he tried it on.

It was too large and settled snugly just above his ears.

"I've got some paper in an old catalog," Pisspot said, digging under the bunk. "Jam some paper in the sweat band and she'll fit just right."

Dirk took a few pages from the mail-order catalog, folded them, and worked them beneath the sweat band, and it was as Pisspot said. The hat fit perfectly.

He stood and cocked the hat. "I'm like a new man."

"Snatched from the bullroachers is our hatted babe, new like the morning sun." Mob did a jig around in a circle. "New, new, new. . . ."

"All you need now is a mule," Pisspot said. "We'll set you on one in the morning. But now, for tonight, I think we ought to celebrate your birthday. If you're borned today like Mob says we ought to have a birthday party for you. Ain't that so, Mob?"

Mob's dancing increased and he began to do a high-step jig with a kick now and then aimed at the hound. The dog got up and slowly walked outside, as if bored by all the noise.

"Seems like I had a jug of panther piss out under the shack," Pisspot said. He went outside and came back in a couple of minutes with a one-gallon crock jug. The cork was driven in so tight he had to pick it out with a pocket knife, and when it was clear he smelled the opening and wrinkled his nose and pulled back.

"Like I said, panther piss." He handed the jug to Dirk who also smelled it—could smell nothing but raw alcohol—and took a short swallow. It was straight, smooth, clean, and clear corn whiskey.

"That's some squeezings," he said, when he'd gotten his breath. He handed the jug to Mob, but Pisspot shook his head and took it instead.

"Mob don't drink. Makes him crazy."

"That stuff would make anybody crazy."

Pisspot took a long draught, crooking the jug over his elbow, then breathed deeply, his eyes watering. "I got it on our last trip out to sell mules, must have been two years ago. I had me some wolf skins and the buyer didn't have any money but he swore it was good. It is, ain't it?"

Dirk took the jug again, swallowed longer this time, holding his breath. He thought briefly that it would be good to sit an evening and listen to Pisspot's stories while tipping the jug, thought about how wonderful these two old men were to give him a hat and a gun and a mule, thought he ought to just relax and lean back and tell them just how goddamn good they were, but the corn liquor—it must have been virtually straight alcohol—combined with the leftover tenderness of the head wound.

Something he wanted to know, he thought,

there was some small thing—oh, yeah, how Piss-pot got his name. "Hey, Pisspot, we know how Mob got named. How about your name, how did that come about?"

But Pisspot didn't answer, just smiled, and in about six minutes Dirk was hammer drunk and two minutes after that his eyes rolled back in his head and he went facedown on the bunk.

Done.

I T was like a nightmare repeated.

Dirk opened his eyes in stages to see that the hound was standing next to him with a sad look on his face. As Dirk saw him the old dog reached out with a slobbery tongue and licked him across the mouth.

"Eccchhh!"

He rolled on his back and sat up, in slow stages. His whole face was wet so the hound must have been licking him for a time and judging by the dents in his face and the way his nose felt bent over he must have lain exactly all night as he'd fallen—facedown.

He was dying of thirst, felt as if his mouth was glued shut, and he made his way—like a doddering blind old man—to the water bucket in the corner and drank out of the dipper. He didn't care that the hound had probably been drinking out of it, didn't care about anything except getting some water down.

"Them as can't hold their liquor shouldn't drink."

Dirk turned slowly to see Pisspot walk in. Mob was in back of him.

"That wasn't liquor," Dirk said. Every word hurt his head. "That was—was something else. It wasn't liquor."

"Them," Mob said, perfectly mimicking Pisspot, "as can't hold their liquor shouldn't drink."

"I won't," Dirk said, drinking more water, drinking more and more water but never enough. "Ever."

"There's cold possum stew on the stove in that pot," Pisspot said. "You should eat. . . ."

Oh, God, yes, Dirk thought—I should eat. Some cold possum stew. Oh, yes. He damn near threw up thinking about it. "Later."

Pisspot nodded. "I figured as much. Well, if you ain't going to eat you might as well come outside. We picked a mule for you and Mob will green it out so's you can ride it."

Dirk followed them out to the corral—or what they called the corral. About fifty yards from the shack they had raised a board lean-to, made—as was the shack—from boards gleaned from old freight wagons they'd found along the trail into the Oklahoma Territory. In front of the lean-to, which in reality was not much cruder than the shack they lived in, they had thrown up a pole fence with rails made of crooked small trees. In the middle they had sunk a snubbing post, made of a ten-inch piece of pine eight feet long, and here they broke the mules. They let the main herd, never more than ten or so, run loose with a stud burro and a mare on rope hobbles so they wouldn't run, and brought them in one at a time to work on them in the "corral."

Dirk had never said it, but he figured the poles wouldn't hold a dead horse, much less an active young mule.

Tied to the snubbing post in the middle of the pen was a large, young mule. It must have been close on sixteen hands and Dirk recognized it as one of the three-year-olds that Pisspot had marked for a special sale to the army—to be sold separately. The mule was extremely well built and Dirk could see his muscles ripple beneath the gray hair and tight skin as he worked against the pressure of the snubbing post.

He was also extremely mad. The two old men had snubbed him down right, so tight his neck was right against the post, and put a blindfold on him to bridle and saddle him, but that hadn't calmed him. He jerked and strained at the snub, his teeth bared and his big ears laid back and Dirk thought, I am a dead man.

"He ain't as bad as he looks," Pisspot said.

Right, Dirk thought—the son of a bitch is a snake. A snake from hell.

"He's been broke and all," Pisspot said, reading Dirk's face. "He's just spirited—a little spirited."

A snake, Dirk thought—a spirited snake from hell.

"Mob will green him out for you."

As he spoke he moved into the corral with Mob following. The two men gave a wide berth to the mule's back legs and the animal's ears followed their movements, locating them by sound. Horses kicked but mules, Dirk knew, aimed their kicks and could kick sideways with precise accuracy. The mule now took a shot at Mob as he came up alongside him, but the old man expertly dodged the hoof and swung up into the saddle and found the off stirrup and nodded to Pisspot.

Pisspot jerked the snubbing rope loose from the post but left it tied to the mule and in the same motion pulled the blindfold off.

The effect was immediate.

The mule—rider, saddle, and whole world—exploded in a cloud of dust as the mule fought to shake Mob off.

He could ride, Dirk thought, watching the mule go insane. Mob was the best he'd ever seen. But the mule was crazy, flat crazy, and he did everything but turn inside out. He sunfished, snapped, tried to rear back over—Mob hit him on the back of the head so hard the snot flew out of the mule's nose—tried to reach around and rip Mob's leg off, snorted, screamed, shook, and tried to roll over.

All at once.

And when none of them worked, when Mob stuck it like a burr—Dirk had never seen a rider so good, at any age—the mule headed for the fence. He tried to scrape Mob off his back but Mob turned him in and in and in until he was circling in the middle of the corral in tight little left circles, and finally, the mule stood, blowing, blood at its nostrils.

"Phew," Dirk realized he'd been holding his breath.

"See?" Pisspot said. "I told you he was broke and just needed to be greened out a bit. Why look, he's gentle as a kitten."

Mob leaned over to the side and spit and Dirk could see part of a tooth come out. Some kitten.

"Why don't you give him a spin now?" Pisspot said. "Just so's you'll get to know each other before you leave."

"Well. . . ." Dirk was wondering how far he'd have to walk to find a horse. There must be somebody in the territory with a horse for sale.

"Sure, climb on up there. You'll see."

Mob threw a leg over the horn and dropped to the ground lightly and handed the hackamore tied to the halter to Dirk.

Well, Dirk thought—they gave me a good hat and a good gun. Two out of three isn't bad. He jammed a foot in the stirrup and swung up, expecting the mule to detonate at any part of any second.

It quivered. The mule hung and quivered beneath him and he tensed, waiting. Seconds passed, then close to a minute, and the mule seemed to quiet, stand, its ears back to listen to him.

Maybe, Dirk thought, maybe Pisspot was right and it would be nice to him. He made sure his tongue wasn't between his teeth—a memory of seeing a man in the army bite his tongue off when a horse bucked on him caused that—raised his heels and lightly dug them into the mule's ribs.

Later he would think of it as dropping a match into a ten-pound keg of powder.

The mule absolutely blew up. It was as if he'd never been bucked out before. He crow-hopped and sunfished and stiff-legged, tried to come back over on him, bite his leg, spun in a circle so tight the world seemed to blur, and Dirk grabbed the horn and stuck it.

It felt like his balls were being driven up into his throat and Dirk still hung on to the horn and stuck it.

Then the mule found something new. Bucking, pounding up and down he worked his way across the corral *into* the lean-to and proceeded to drive every board off the roof with Dirk's head.

On the fourth buck Dirk caught a rafter and broke it with his shoulder, saw dust showering down on him, then took another shot on top of his head and saw only sky through the open roof up between his spread legs as he left the mule's back and landed in a lump of arms and legs and cuts and bruises in the mule shit in the corner of the lean-to.

"Damn," Pisspot said, pulling him to his feet while Mob caught the mule. "Don't you just love a spirited animal?"

I probably wouldn't have to walk more than two, three hundred miles before I found a horse, Dirk thought, when he *could* think. His brain kept flopping like a fish dying on a riverbank. "Look, it's probably not right, me taking your best mule and all. . . ."

"Pshaw! Don't you worry none." Pisspot led him back over to the mule. "Little green bucking like that's to show you he's a good one. Here, I'll help you back up."

No, Dirk thought. Don't. Please.

But to his horror he saw his foot—was it really his foot?—going into the stirrup and his leg swinging over the saddle and his butt slamming down and he thought, Well, I'll just die here and that's the end of it.

And the mule didn't buck.

It stood beneath him for a moment, flies coming in to investigate the foam at the sides of its mouth, and shook its ears and farted and didn't buck.

Dirk held his breath, raised his heels, and dug them in.

The mule moved forward and left and right and held for him and didn't buck. He dismounted, remounted, slapping the animal on the neck, dug his heels in harder, and still it didn't buck.

"Open the gate," he said, and Mob swung the two poles wide. He rode the mule out, across the stream and up the hill, brought it up to a canter, then a full run on a flat meadow above the shack, and it took it all as if it had been running under him all its life.

"It has a smooth run," Dirk said when he got back to the corral and the waiting old men. "Smoothest I've ever seen and it seems to have a lot of bottom—though I didn't ride it far enough to know."

"I told you," Pisspot said, smiling with his gums and tobacco-stained lips wide. "That's a good mule. We wouldn't of stuck you on a bad one." Mob whispered something in his ear and he smiled and nodded. "Oh, yeah, I forgot to tell you—the saddle is for you, too. Goes with the mule."

Dirk dismounted and stood, holding the hackamore. "I can ride bareback. . . ."

"No. You can't. Not as far as you want to go. You take the saddle—we got two more. Besides, I hate them western rigs. Give me a light army saddle any day. . . ."

Which was a lie and they both knew it, but Dirk said nothing for a moment. Hell, he thought, I really *am* like a babe in the bullrushes. I wouldn't have anything without these two—I'd be dead. "I guess I'll be going before you give me everything you have."

Pisspot nodded. "I figured that—come on, we'll help you with your gear."

Dirk thought, What gear, but he tied the mule off and turned to follow Pisspot, but out of the corner of his eye he saw Mob dab at his cheeks with his sleeve, sniffle and turn away, and he thought there were worse things than having an old man sorry to see you leave.

C·H·A·P·T·E·R

☆ —————— 6 —————— ☆

DIRK raised himself in the saddle. The sweat had worked through the dirty trousers and he was sticking to the leather and cloth.

The mule was stopped on a ridge overlooking a shallow dish of land perhaps six or seven miles across. On the other side was a similar ridge and he expected to see another one when he crossed that ridge and then another and another.

He'd been doing what he thought of as the goddamn ridges for the three days since he'd left the old men. The country was green but there had been no rain and it was fast drying off. The grass was belly deep on the mule and the travel was easy enough for all the climbing and dropping on the ridges and he had eased back into covering miles well enough.

His butt was sore the first day but that was natural after not riding for better than two weeks. From then on it was just a matter of learning the fine points of the mule—which proved to be at least as good as both Pisspot and Mob had said he would be—and settling back into routine.

He took the bowler off and wiped his forehead with a sleeve, let the small breeze cool the sweat from his face before replacing the hat. On his side the Walker jerked at him, almost pulled him over and he eased the weight. He toyed with the idea of hanging the gun from the horn but remembered the last time he'd gotten separated from his Colt and decided against it. If the mule dumped him and took off, he'd have no gun, and he wasn't about to be without a gun again.

"Not that you'd dump me, would you, hammer brain?" he said aloud. The mule's ears twitched and rolled back, listening to him, but it didn't move.

Dirk was amazed by the mule. He'd seen many of them in the army and had heard all the stories about how tough, how smart, how much better than horses they were but had never really believed them. All he knew of them before this was watching the teamsters crack their whips over them and seeing bits of meat come off their ears from the tips on the snake whips and the long-winded roar of obscenities it seemed to take to get them going. Some of the teamsters, it was said, could swear for twenty minutes straight without repeating themselves.

But this mule was giving him an education.

It was smart, tough as old iron, and hadn't balked once. At one point, as they were crossing a small patch of round rocks, the mule's foot had come down within two feet of a sunning rattlesnake. The snake instantly set up a buzz and where a horse would have gone crazy and probably dumped him the mule just stepped calmly sideways twice—almost a dance—until it was out of strike range, then resumed walking.

It had a slightly rough but mile-eating trot and as Dirk had seen initially the smoothest run he'd ever felt on an animal.

"You're just grease, aren't you?" he said aloud again, watching the mule's ears. They seemed to be mounted on swivels and rotated round and round independent of each other.

They now slammed forward and Dirk felt the hair come up on his neck.

The mule was hearing something new, something that took his interest, and in the three days of riding Dirk had only seen him do that three times—every time for horses. He had not seen any people in his riding west, though he was back on the general trail he'd been following when he got taken by the scavengers, but he'd seen horses—

apparently wild—three times and each time the mule had heard them or seen them first and his ears had whipped forward as they did now.

"Goddamn shame when a man gets worried just because he thinks there might be a horse about," Dirk said, but his hand fell naturally on the Dragoon at his belt.

Except this time it wasn't a horse. He now heard the sound the mule had first heard—the metallic pinging of metal being struck against metal a long way off. The sound of a hammer and anvil.

He studied the basin before him again but could see nothing that resembled a settlement. The trail wound down from the ridge and out across the bottom of the basin through small stands of willows and stunted pine—almost brush. The pinging seemed to be coming from no specific point, rather all over the basin, but that meant nothing. Sound could do funny things in a big dish like this.

About a mile and a half below and ahead there was a stand of cottonwoods along what appeared to be a small creek, and Dirk thought that might be the source of the sound.

Whatever it was the mule took it as a signal to get moving and it began to move forward and down from the ridge.

Dirk let him pick his way, leaned back in the saddle to ease his weight and help the mule's balance, and at the bottom as they came out in the basin he stopped again. He hadn't heard anything over the clatter of the rocks on the mule's hooves, but as soon as they stopped he heard the sound again, louder now, and he could tell that it was indeed coming from the cottonwoods on the creek.

"Probably a ranch," he said to the mule, and felt his mouth water. If it was a ranch, he could hit them for a meal and maybe a pair of jeans or overalls. When he'd left Pisspot had handed him a sack of beans, a thick iron kettle, a slab of bacon and half a pound of Arbuckles, all of which he'd tied to his saddle in a feed sack. He'd used a rock to smash the coffee beans in a rag for coffee, and he didn't want to think or seem ungrateful—the old men had given him more than he thought he'd ever have when he was looking down the bore of the Greener—but he was sick to death of beans and salt pork.

If it was a ranch, he might hit them up for a meal. He let his mind run with it. Maybe they'd be having steak or beef stew; maybe they had some spuds and they'd have steak and beef stew and biscuits and he could eat his fill and give his ass and the mule's ears a rest from the goddamn beans. Sometimes it felt like he was spending more time above the saddle than in it.

The mule made his own way out into the basin but before they were halfway to the cottonwoods the pinging sound came to a stop. Yet there were other sounds now. Dirk heard chickens and that set his mouth to watering again. Maybe they'd have chicken and spuds and he could use the chicken juice on the potatoes or maybe they'd even have a cook who made gravy and biscuits and he could sop the biscuits in gravy and clean his plate with them. . . .

There was a sudden crack and a bullet passed close to his ear.

His body took over and he was rolling out of the saddle before he truly realized he was being shot at, and he was on his feet in back of the mule with the Walker out looking over the top of the saddle before his thinking was properly off chicken and gravy and biscuits.

It had been close. He'd heard the snap of the slug going by his ear so it must have been within a foot or so.

There was a cloud of smoke half as big as a granary at the edge of the cottonwoods and for a moment Dirk stood looking at it. It was well over a hundred yards to the smoke and he thought, Hell, I'd have to shoot the Walker three times to get there. . . .

"Hello the house," he yelled, thinking it might be a mistake. He could see no house but he was certain there was a ranch headquarters or house in the trees. Although after the shot the chickens had grown quiet and there was no other indication of people. Except of course for the cloud of smoke from the gun. There was that—the smoke.

There was no answer.

"I'm just passing through and don't mean any harm," he yelled again. He was encouraged that no second shot seemed to be coming but felt distinctly uncomfortable standing out in the open. It was just like goddamn Gettysburg, he thought—nothing in front of you but air. Somebody told him later the battle started because some Johnnies went looking for shoes to cover their feet and ran into a picket line and then Yanks and Johnnies just kept coming and coming. . . .

"My name is Prine," he yelled. "Duncan Prine."

"Well, you ride right on around, Mr. Duncan Pine, or I'll give you a new belly button."

Well, hell, Dirk thought, it's nothing but a kid. The voice was high—his nuts hadn't dropped yet. Just a shaver. Then he remembered the Johnnies. Lots of them were young and they'd put a ball in you in a heartbeat.

"I need to water my mule," he yelled back. He returned the Walker to its holster to show he meant no harm, glad now that he hadn't tried to shoot back. "I won't be bothering you for anything else."

"I *know* that," came the voice, a smart edge to it. "You ain't bothering *me* at all."

Not just a kid, Dirk thought, but a cocky kid. It reminded him of himself when he was young. Once he ate a mouthful of poison ivy just to show his mother how tough he was and that it wouldn't bother him—they had to feed him through a copper tube in the side of his mouth for a week and a half. Smart. Or maybe it was just that the kid was scared.

Dirk raised his arms, held the reins loosely from the mule, and led him as he walked toward the cottonwoods. He could see now through the cloud of smoke and there were some willows at the edge of the cottonwoods and as he moved he could see a small cabin back in the trees.

The kid was in the willows and Dirk walked straight to them. As he got close he could see the barrel of a rifle sticking out of the willows, aimed at about roughly his middle.

He stopped twenty yards from the willows. The barrel didn't waver, held on him steady. A cocky kid, Dirk thought, who could kill me so easy now it would be like swatting a fly.

"I'll just get some water for my mule," Dirk said. "If you'll allow it."

"Pump's by the stock shed," the voice said—Dirk still could not see the boy. "You get water and then you get gone."

From the barrel Dirk could tell the rifle was a muzzle loader, although he couldn't see if it was cap or flint. No matter. The hole was the same.

"Maybe you'd better go tell your ma or pa I'm here—they might get upset me coming right up to the pump with no warning."

Dirk knew there weren't any parents—they'd have been out by now—but the edge of a suspicion was coming and he wanted to find out if it was true.

"They ain't here right now," the boy said. "But that don't matter. You get your ass to the pump and water that Missouri mudhen and get on your way."

Dirk did as he was told but he could hear the hardness going in the boy's voice. He let the mule drink—noting it was less than a horse would drink after half a day of those ridges. No, he thought, those goddamn ridges.

It was a small place, but neat enough. A cabin and a stock shed with a pole corral, a chicken coop at the end of the shed—little more than an added box on the end of the building—completed the yard. There were no horses, no cattle, no other stock. The cabin had a burned corner, a smear of black where somebody had fired it and it went out. Or was put out. The pump was in the middle of the opening between the cabin and the stock shed. There were pretty curtains with flowers on them in the two windows of the cabin.

Shit, Dirk thought—they came here. The sons of bitches came here and somehow missed the boy. He stood with his back to the well and

trough and pumped for the mule to drink. He
took a drink himself, a long, cool one, then
washed his face with water and thought again—
the sons of bitches were here. That's what happened to the boy's ma and pa.

"Boy," he said, without turning to face the willows. "What's your name?"

"It don't matter none to you but it's Tilden.
Tilden Holmes."

"Your ma and pa aren't coming home, are
they?"

"Yes they are, too. They'll be home directly."
But there was a break in his voice and Dirk knew
he was lying.

He let the mule drink, long draughts because
he knew he wasn't going to be riding him on right
away. He turned to face the willows, knowing the
boy wouldn't shoot. Correction, he thought, hoping the boy wouldn't shoot.

"Did some men come through here two, three
weeks ago and raise a lot of hell?"

Silence from the willows.

"There would have been three or four of
them," he said. "One named Carley and maybe
one named Shaver."

"Four," the boy said. "There was four of the
bastards and one of them limped like he'd been
hurt."

"That would have been Shaver. I put a bullet

in him—or thought I did. Things happened kind of fast."

"I was going to shoot them but I would only have gotten one and then they would have gotten me so I didn't shoot." It all came out in a rush. "I'd been downstream in some low brush hunting because Pa wanted a deer and sometimes there was deer come into that brush to eat the dirt. There is something in the dirt they want to eat down there. I was there and waiting for a deer when I heard the shots and by the time I got back to the house it was too late, too late. . . ."

He broke off for a minute and Dirk could hear him crying in the willows—still couldn't see him. He leaned to tie the mule off, then walked toward the willows, and when he got closer could see the figure of a boy under some low limbs, back in.

A small boy.

"Friends call me Dirk," he said, standing next to the willows. "Why don't you come out of there, Tilden? Those same bastards left me for dead and took everything I owned."

The boy stood and when he was up Dirk could tell he was only twelve. Maybe thirteen. The rifle was an old Civil War sniper rifle with a bull barrel and an adjustable peep sight that must have weighed close to twelve pounds—the gun was bigger than the boy. It was the kind of rifle that could shoot bullets or balls, either one, and take a man out at four or five hundred yards. A lot of gun for the boy to shoot.

There were streaks down his cheeks from tears and he wiped them with a sleeve, let the rifle butt down to the ground. He was skinny but that might have come from not eating right for the last two weeks. Kids were like pups. Dirk knew that from the war, seeing them when the Johnnies had taken all their food. They'd grow fat or skinny while you watched them. He was wearing an old felt hat that hung down over his eyes and made his ears fold over but under and around the edge of the hat Dirk could see the ends of red hair. Bright red hair.

"They had already shot Pa," the boy continued after he caught his breath, "and when Ma tried to keep them from Ellie one of them shot her too and I sat here in the willows and watched them and there wasn't nothing I could do. . . ."

"Who is Ellie?" Dirk almost said *was*, not who *is* Ellie.

"Ellie is my sister. They took her with them, although why I can't see. She's ugly as a trough bottom. Real tall and skinny with red hair and freckles thick as lice. I wouldn't think a man would even look at her, let alone want to take her with him. They stuck her on Old Puller—he was our workhorse—and made her ride bareback and laughed and joked about what they were going to do to her that night when they camped. One of them kept touching her on the chest, grabbing at her, said as how big they were and all. I'm surprised they got her on the horse, the way she fought—caught one of them in the gourds so bad he hung on his saddle horn and puked."

He was winding down now. It was as if he'd had all this bottled up inside and was just waiting for someone to tell it to.

"They tried to fire the cabin but it didn't take right and when they were gone I threw a little water on it and it went right out. Then they tried to catch the chickens but couldn't. They tore the insides of the cabin up some, looking for things— I don't know what they expected to find—and then they was gone. It's like Pa says—used to say—gone like a bad wind."

He took another breath. Dirk was going to ask how long it had been, exactly, but before he got the question in the boy started again.

"I buried Ma and Pa on that low rise west of the cabin. They used to like to go up there and have an evening cup of coffee so I thought they'd like that—be where they could see all around. Ma was real light but Pa was big and it took me most of an hour to get him to the holes. He was big, my pa, real big, and they just shot him and shot him. . . ."

He started crying now and before Dirk knew what was happening the boy had come forward and dropped the rifle and was leaning against his leg, crying and crying, and Dirk put his hand on the boy's shoulder and patted him and wanted to tell him it was all right.

But it wasn't.

No part of it was all right for the boy and he let him cry, standing in the evening sun, looking at the low rise to the west where the boy had buried his parents, and thought about a bad wind.

It was strange how things seemed to fit, Dirk thought, currying and wiping the mule. It was as if he were the same as the kid's pa somehow. He'd put the mule in the shed and found a small sack of oats and given the mule some and when he went to look for a currycomb he'd just reached and there it was—right where his hand went to find it.

Once over his fear the boy was glad to see somebody. He'd been alone for close to three weeks and when he knew Dirk meant no harm he nearly talked Dirk's ear off.

"We didn't have nothing when we came here," he said, sounding all grown-up though Dirk knew he was aping his father. By the looks of the logs in the cabin and the stock shed they'd been here a time—at least ten years. That meant the kid was probably only two or three when they first settled, or maybe even born here, and he couldn't remember what it had been like.

"Pa, he had an ax and a single-bore shotgun and

Ma had a saucepan and a billy pot and that was about it and they made it."

"How many chickens are there?" Dirk asked. He still had thoughts of a meal that didn't include beans and salt pork. "And are there any spuds?"

The boy nodded. He was standing in the doorway to the stock shed while Dirk finished brushing the mule with a sack and the currycomb and put him out in the pen.

"We got a root cellar them bastards didn't find and there's spuds and some p'serves Ma has— had—up and we don't need the chickens anyway."

"You don't?" This was a new turn and Dirk stopped to look at the boy. "Why not?"

"Well, hell." His swearing didn't work quite right. "We can't take them with us, can we?"

"Us?"

"What else? It's plain as dirt you're riding after them and I've got to get Ellie back, don't I? You think I *ain't* riding out of here with you?" He drew himself up to his full height—about halfway to Dirk's shoulder—and shrugged. "Besides, two guns are better than one. Especially when all you've got is that short gun. It 'pears you *need* somebody like me."

Dirk rubbed his neck. It was suddenly stiff. And his head hurt a little from the wound— though it was completely healed now. He took the derby off and used his sleeve to wipe sweat from his head and thought about what he had facing him.

He couldn't take the boy. Whatever happened when and if he caught up with them it wasn't going to be a place for a pup—even a tough pup who could shoot a rifle. And as to saving Ellie—he didn't want to say it but chances were good that Ellie was already dead or left for dead in some crib, tied in a back room. He'd seen that too in the war.

Women and kids, he thought, women and kids always took the worst of it.

"I know what you're thinking," the boy said. "But you ain't leaving me here. I'm going to get those bastards."

Then too, Dirk thought, there's nothing but the mule. They hadn't left a horse for the boy and Dirk wasn't sure he could ride the mule double, or if he could for how long. On the other hand the boy was right—he couldn't really leave him here. There were men riding now, like the men who came through and killed his pa and ma, who would take the boy and use him and it was just a matter of time until they came.

He walked to the pump, the boy following, and drank water and splashed more in his face again. There wasn't a way out of this.

"Why don't you kill a chicken and we'll pluck it and boil some spuds," Dirk said. "And I'd love some salt if you got some. I haven't had salt in close on a month and I miss it."

The boy nodded. He put the rifle inside the door of the cabin and caught a chicken and wrung the neck expertly—a quick flick of his right hand. Dirk went into the cabin and found it surprisingly neat. The boy was taking care of himself. Better, he thought, smiling, than Pisspot and Mob.

There was a wood stove and he fired it up—feeling the heat immediately fill the tight cabin—and found a large pot to put on to boil water for scalding the chicken.

It took half an hour to get the water hot and Dirk used the time to find some clothes. His own, which Pisspot had given him, were little more than rags and just three days on the trail had turned them worse. They were nearly falling off him.

"Tilden," he said, "I know it maybe don't sound proper just yet but if your pa left some jeans and maybe a shirt that would fit me I'd be forever grateful for the use of them."

"There's no proper to it," the boy said. "Clothes are clothes and men are men. Pa wouldn't mind. If he were here, he'd probably give them to you. Look in that box by the wall there. Those bastards messed things up, but I spent some time putting things back as they were."

Dirk went to where the boy pointed. There was

a large pine box, beautifully cut and fit, and the lid came up evenly. "It's well worked—the wood."

"My pa, he was a carpenter back in Ohio before he come out here. He would of stayed there but except for the dirty banks took everything everybody had and they had to leave. Pa hated the dirty banks."

Inside the box there were some blue work shirts made of heavy material and canvas trousers. Dirk took one of each and changed clothes and was gratified to see that they fit. The shirt was loose in the shoulders and the pants just a bit snug, but they were close and would break in with wear and the saddle.

He dug farther in the box and found a pair of boots. He held them up. They were oiled leather, looked to be fine leather, and soft, with a medium heel. He pulled the work brogans off his feet and tried the boots and was gratified to see that they almost fit. They were just a shade loose across the wide part of his foot but he found some socks and with the socks on the boots felt about right.

"We must have been close to the same size," Dirk said, "your pa and me."

"No." The boy's voice was flat. "There wasn't nobody like my pa. Nobody."

Dirk turned to see that the boy was crying again, without knowing it. He nodded. "I can see that—he must have been something, your pa."

This time the boy said nothing, just nodded.

The water came to a boil and Dirk took the pan outside. He dunked the dead chicken in and swirled it around to soak all the feathers and began to pluck while the boy went back into the cabin and came out with six big potatoes.

Dirk could not smell wet feathers without thinking of home and his mother working at plucking chickens—she always seemed to be plucking chickens—in the backyard. They had lived with nothing, the Prines. There simply wasn't money, but she was always plucking chickens and they always ate.

He wondered suddenly what he would have done faced with what this boy had come at him—see his ma and pa shot and sister taken off.

Christ, he thought, looking at the boy peeling potatoes—what could he do with the kid? "Tilden, do you have family somewhere? Or somebody your pa and ma knew where you could go?"

The boy looked at him with a sideways squint, the hat making a shelf over his eyes. Dirk thought that he'd seen the look before and then almost smiled when he remembered it was Pisspot—the same curious study.

"It won't wash," the boy said, shaking his head. "You ain't dumping me until we get to them. After they're dead and Ellie's back you can do what you want—but now you ain't dumping me."

"Well, hell, boy," Dirk heard the exasperation in his voice, "you can't come with me. You ain't got a horse and I haven't got but the one mule."

"I can run alongside. I did it with Old Puller lots of times. Just hang on a strap and run. . . ."

He was asking now, begging, and it struck Dirk that what the boy was begging for was to be able to kill some men. Like he was begging for candy. Catch up and kill them. His eyes had the pleading look of all children when they wanted something—or pups, for that matter.

Begging to kill.

"We'll come at it another time," Dirk said, dropping it. "Let's cook the chicken and spuds. I can't remember when I've had but beans and belly."

They went into the cabin and Dirk cut the chicken in pieces to cook in a covered pan. He found some lard in a can and salt—God, he thought, salt—and he put both in for taste.

The boy put the potatoes in a pot with some water to boil and they went back outside. The stove was roaring now, and in the small cabin and with the summer heat it became almost unbearable.

"Here's how we'll work it," the boy said as soon as they were in the sunlight and cooler air. "I'll run alongside you hanging on a strap until we catch up with them. Then even if we don't get all of them we can kill at least one and get his horse for me to ride while we get the rest."

"Right." Dirk remembered them coming up on him, Shaver talking about killing him as if it were a present. The smile in the man's eyes when he popped the cap on him. We'll catch up and kill one of them and take his horse. Right.

"No," Dirk said, shaking his head. "That isn't 'how we'll work it.' " He had taken a pinch of salt in his mouth in the cabin and it made him thirsty so he walked to the pump to drink. "You can ride with me until we get to the next ranch where there's decent folks that can take in a pup and there you will stay. Hell, I don't know where these men went or what I'll do when—*if*—I catch them. They've got a three-week edge on me now and if they push it at all I probably won't see them until California. If then."

Dirk expected the boy to fight and was surprised to see that he seemed to accept what Dirk had said. He didn't nod, but seemed to shrug and went back to the cabin porch to sit and wriggle a toe in the dirt. He was barefoot and his feet looked impossibly dirty and Dirk thought how fast a boy could go down without a mother and then naturally thought of Pisspot and Mob. Any woman, he thought. Men just went down and down without them.

The smell coming out of the cabin rolled over him and the salt and lard and baking chicken

mixed with the light smell from the boiling potatoes just about drove him crazy with hunger.

"You figure that chicken is done enough to
eat?" he said to the boy.

"Never eat chicken raw," Tilden answered.
"Ma says—said—it gives you the shits and blind
staggers. She didn't say it that way, of course, but
that's what she meant."

"Well, I'll tell you, Tilden, I'm just about to
the point where I'm so hungry I wouldn't care if
I *did* get a little blind staggers. Let's eat."

C·H·A·P·T·E·R

☆ ——————— 7 ——————— ☆

"**L**ET'S give it a rest."

Dirk stopped the mule and reached around to slide the boy off the side and down to the ground. Tilden rode well, and the mule took the extra weight with no complaints—Dirk was more and more amazed by the animal—but he wasn't taking any chances on blowing the mule up.

The boy slid easily to the ground, though the barrel of the old sniper rifle caught Dirk in the head on the way down. "Had to bring that cannon, didn't you?"

Tilden squinted up at him. " 'Pears you can't talk all that much about cannons, what with that hog you're carrying."

Dirk smiled but said nothing. The kid gave as

good as he got and in truth Dirk was coming to like him. They'd come two days from the ranch, spent one night camped by a small stream, and the boy was handy to have around.

As soon as Dirk had pulled the mule to a stop the night before—let him stop, would be more like it—the boy was on the ground and gathering wood for a fire. While Dirk was busting coffee beans and getting a pot of water going, the boy was off in the brush, and in ten or fifteen minutes Dirk heard the big rifle belch and Tilden came back with a brush rabbit, the head neatly blown almost away.

"You hit him that way by accident?" Dirk had asked, knowing the answer.

"So's I wouldn't ruin the meat—Pa always said to shoot things where you can't eat." He expertly dropped the guts from the rabbit while he talked, washed the carcass in the stream, cut it in pieces with a folding knife, and had a stew of rabbit and three potatoes they'd brought from the ranch—almost all before Dirk was properly settled in camp.

Dirk swung his leg over the mule and lowered to the ground, walked along leading the animal with the boy walking on the other side of his head.

They were in some rolling hills—little more than slow rises—and the grass was close to waist high. Dirk let the mule walk slowly, gauging his speed to him so he would rest. Another trick from the army. He'd been in the infantry but had met a cavalry sergeant and drank some skull-thud with him and the sergeant had shared wisdom with him. "Always set your goddamned movement to the goddamned horse's goddamned thinking and you'll be all goddamned right," the sergeant had said, laced with even more obscenities than Dirk remembered. And he'd been right. A horse doesn't ride a man, a man rides a horse. Simple thinking. Later he heard the sergeant had a ball come in one ear and go out the other and stop his thinking for him, but Dirk thought of him now and then.

"Where you from?" Tilden asked suddenly.

Dirk spit and stooped to scratch at a chigger bite. They had worked in around his boot tops and itched like blazes. "Back in Pennsylvania. A small red-dirt farm that couldn't grow gut beans. My pa and ma were poor. . . ."

He remembered how poor. Crawling under the bed once to hide from his brother and looking up in the slats at rags hidden there; rags that his mother used for her monthlies when she had any, when she wasn't pregnant. Rags she had to use over. Poor. So poor his father couldn't afford harness leather for the one horse they owned and had to use rope.

Poor from the drinking his father did.

Jesus, he hated being poor.

"You never said where you were from—I just thought I'd ask."

Dirk let it die there. He didn't talk much about the army or the war and he didn't talk much about the dirt farm in Pennsylvania because he didn't like to think about either one of them.

"Don't this country grow long?" Tilden said after a few more steps. He was barefoot and the chiggers didn't seem to bother him. Nothing seemed to bother him, Dirk thought—kid tough. His pa would have been proud of him. God damn them, to ride in and just kill and take that way. God damn them.

They walked up a shallow incline in the grass and as they crested it Dirk saw some dark spots ahead of them, close to half a mile away. They barely showed over the next low rise but even at that distance and partially hidden he could tell what they were.

"Buffalo," Dirk said, but the boy was way ahead of him.

"I saw them. We had them come through the place a couple of times but Pa said hunters were starting to push them back. Good thing, too. Four of them hit the garden and Ma like to bust her bustle. You should of seen her, chasing a bull with a frying pan. She hit him, too. Three, four times." The boy smiled but Dirk saw his eyes tear up. "Ma was something. . . ."

"I was thinking," Dirk said quickly, to change

the subject, "that it might be good to sit down to some steak. Do you think you could see about taking one of them with that long gun of yours?"

Tilden nodded. "Like shooting a cabin."

"Take a small cow," Dirk said. "The meat is better and we won't waste so much. I'll wait here until I hear you shoot."

Again Tilden nodded and set off ahead at an easy trot. He was soon out of sight and Dirk stopped walking. The mule stopped with him.

A long time passed—it seemed longer for the waiting. Flies came to the mule when they quit moving and it stamped at them, flicked its tail. Dirk slapped at a couple of them, brushed the mule's head to keep them away.

He could see the buffalo—at least their backs showing over the rise—dark, solid lumps against the gray-green grass—but not the boy, who seemed to have been swallowed up by the country.

Two of the buffalo on the right seemed to move nervously—though it was too far to tell accurately—and just when he thought the boy had messed it up he heard the dull thud-boom of a rifle at a distance and one of the buffalo dropped into the grass.

"Steaks," he said to the mule. He swung into the saddle and let the mule trot forward and had gone perhaps two steps when there was another shot.

Then another, and another and more—the sequence of shots much too close for the boy to be reloading the long gun.

It was more than one person shooting and the first thing that came to mind was Indians. He had not heard of them this far south—until you got into Comanches on down in Texas—but where there were buffalo there could be Indians.

Higher on the mule he could see the buffalo drop with the shots and in a few moments he realized it couldn't be Indians. The shooting was evenly paced, and he could see no riders, no people at all—just the mystery guns dropping the buffalo one by one, thudding on the prairie grass. Had it been Indians he thought they would be riding among the buffalo and just when he thought that he saw the boy.

He was trotting back toward Dirk through the grass, the rifle hanging loosely at his side. He came to a stop near Dirk's stirrup.

"Hunters," the boy said. His breathing was deep but even and Dirk thought he could probably run for a week. "I saw their wagon down in a low place. I couldn't tell how many there were but there must be more than one."

Dirk nodded, dismounted. He was not sure of the direction of shooting but buffalo hunters shot big guns and the slugs carried. Old habits die hard and the army taught him low was better. Always.

The shooting continued and he watched the

buffalo dropping. They milled some but held for it until half the small herd, about twenty animals, had been killed. Then a bad shot caught one of them in the gut and it grunted—they could hear it from where they stood watching—and broke and ran, its tail slammed down over its ass and its belly hunched around the hit.

The strange run spooked the rest of the herd and they broke and ran with the wounded animal. Even when it dropped in a couple of hundred yards the rest kept on until they were past the fallen buffalo. The firing followed them and there may have been more hits but no further animals dropped, and when they crossed over a low rise the firing stopped.

There were clouds of smoke from another rise, past where the herd had been grazing when they got hit, and Dirk debated riding toward it. Hunters could be rough people and they might not take kindly to Dirk and the boy coming up on them.

"I never saw them," the boy said, as if reading his mind. "But the wagon looked new. It's a high-side freight wagon, painted red. . . ."

"Red?"

Tilden nodded. "Red, with white lines and a new tarp. I don't think they're just hiders."

Dirk mounted and reached down for the boy, who easily clambered up in back of him. "Well, they can sure as hell spare us some meat—they must have ten ton of it waiting for the flies."

"Don't seem right, somehow," Tilden said from in back of him as the mule started up. "Just shooting them that way for their hides."

Dirk shook his head. "There's no right and no wrong to it. To anything. There just is. We can't have buffalo anymore—they don't mix with gardens and farms. Like what happened to your ma's garden. I've heard stories of herds up north that take a week to pass, a week and more. Think what that would do to a garden."

"Still—it don't seem right. . . ."

Dirk could see the wagon now and figures moving and the boy was right. The wagon was red, bright red, red as Maggie's drawers. When he was a hundred and fifty yards from the wagon he stopped the mule and raised in the saddle and waved and yelled. He didn't want them mistaken for a buffalo.

One of the men, near the wagon, saw them and waved back, and they rode on in.

There was a team of horses on the wagon—a young, good-looking set of gelded bays—that must have cost a small ranson, Dirk thought, letting the mule slow and smell them. And the boy was right—the wagon was new. Dusty, but obviously new; the tarp over the high-side bed hardly faded.

As they rode up the man who had waved back at Dirk was unhooking the team from the wagon and heading them toward the buffalo.

There were three men. The one with the horses was wearing weathered clothes and an old flop hat and had a beard. He nodded with his chin as he passed Dirk and Tilden, but the team was jerking him along on his feet and he couldn't take a hand loose.

"Got to get to skinning them while they're still loose," he said, and spit tobacco juice to the side.

Dirk nodded and turned to the other two men. They were wearing suits.

"I'll be damned," Tilden said in back of him. He'd been looking under Dirk's armpit. "They come from a catalog. . . ."

And they did look that way—like they'd just stepped out of the pages of a catalog. They had dark suits on and ribbon ties and were wearing wide-brim dark hats. They were both thin, looked almost alike with long cheeks and noses—the cheeks so long they looked flat on the sides. The two of them were holding new rifles—they looked like Sharps—and on their suits the shoulders had recoil pads sewn into the cloth in a little pattern of diamond stitches and Dirk thought, Jesus Christ, where did they come from?

"Oh, I say, hello." One of the men was slightly taller than the other and he now stepped forward. "Hail, fellow, well met."

English, Dirk thought. He'd met some English officers in the army, over to study the war, or heard them, and they sounded much the same as this man. "Hello."

"Please get down and take some refreshments with us. And your boy, as well." He had not at first seen Tilden, who was hidden in back of Dirk on the mule. Tilden slid over and off the mule, dropping lightly to the ground, and Dirk dismounted.

"Our man will be busy skinning the brutes we killed for a time so we won't have any food. But we can offer you tea, if you wish, or something stronger."

"God damn," Tilden said next to Dirk, "have you ever heard the beat of that?"

"Mind your manners," Dirk said, and was surprised to find that he sounded like his mother. God, four days with the kid and he already sounded like a wet nurse.

"I'm Clarence," the Englishman said, ignoring Tilden's comments, "and this is my brother Harold. Clarence and Harold Westchester."

Dirk introduced himself, then turned to the boy. "And this punkin seed is Tilden Holmes."

"So he's not your boy?"

Dirk shook his head. "His folks were killed by scavengers and we're . . ." He trailed off, not wishing to go any further. "Have you seen four men and a woman traveling?" These men seemed so out of place, so ridiculous, that he felt like he was speaking to a set of store dummies.

"Oh, I say, that's tragic," Clarence said. Harold nodded and murmured something condescending. "We haven't seen anybody for close to a month."

Dirk turned to watch "their man" begin to work skinning the buffalo. He was just approaching the first one. Dirk turned back to the Englishman.

"What we really wanted was some meat. Would you mind if we took some off that young cow he's working on?"

"Of course not—there's meat and to spare. This will all be carrion tomorrow. We usually take the tongue and perhaps a hump and leave the rest. Take what you need."

Dirk nodded and motioned to Tilden. The two of them led the mule—which was a little nervous at the blood smell but followed them easily enough—to where the man with the team was beginning work.

He had cut a circle around the dead buffalo's neck and was cutting a long cut from this circle down the middle of the belly to the anus. He looked up briefly when Dirk and Tilden walked up but kept working while he talked.

"I see you met my hunting partners."

Dirk nodded. "Quite the pair to draw to."

"Jesus, I guess." He shook his head, the knife sliding easily through the soft belly skin. There were layers of thick yellow fat beneath the skin.

"Man gets down on his luck oncet in a while but I never thought I would come to this. Jesus H. Christ I didn't."

He looked up suddenly. "My name is Dick. Dick Harris."

"How did you get involved with those two?" Dirk looked back to the wagon where the two Englishmen had taken a couple of folding wooden camp chairs down from the wagon and had spread a fly tarp to provide shade. They were sitting in their chairs in the shade watching "their man" skin.

"It was the devil," Harris said, "the devil singled me out. He always has, ever since I was old enough to know. I was in St. Joe and I had some money and there were the devil's women and the devil's brew and I drank and partook of the devil's women until I had nothing but puking and a sore tool. I can't never get away from the devil. And just when I thought things couldn't get any worse the devil sent them two after me."

He gestured with a bloody hand. "They found me sitting outside the Emporium in St. Joe and told me they want to 'go hunting for hides,' " he made his voice English and toffish. "Come all the way over from England to 'go hunting for hides.' Called it a 'great adventure,' like it was some kind of game. And lord for the money. Jesus, they must *sleep* in money. All new wagon and knives and clothes and guns. They bought three new Sharps

.50-90s and all the loading equipment. If I just *looked* at something they'd go and buy it. Who wouldn't go with them? Who wouldn't?''

Dirk shook his head. "I see what you mean."

But Tilden, who had been standing there, cut in. "I don't see where it's so bad. They gave you money and work, didn't they?"

"Made me a third partner," Harris said, nodding, looking at the boy. "And all I do is what I would have done anyway—shoot and skin critters. And I cook a meal now and again for them. But God *damn* it, I hate their airs and ways and I just got a bad feeling about it all. It just don't sit right, doing this with them. It's like they're just killing for the fun of it, not because they need the money from the hides. They sit in their goddamn chairs and shoot and it's all just a game."

All the time he was speaking he was working. He made the neck and belly cut and peeled some of the neck skin back about a foot. In this he cut a hole and worked a six-foot piece of chain through the hole. He hooked this chain to the doubletree in back of the team, which had been standing placidly waiting for him to get ready.

When the chain was hooked to the team he made a squeaking sound with his lips. The team lunged forward—startling the mule; Dirk had to hold on to him to keep him from bolting—and the buffalo's skin ripped neatly off with a massive sticky tearing sound. The inside of the skin was pink-white in the sun and the flies came in hordes to both the skin and the carcass.

"They won't even rub salt," he said, easing the team and spreading the hide. "I have to do it all. Skin them, salt them—all of it."

"We need some meat," Dirk said. "Is it all right to take it off this cow?" He indicated the carcass on the ground.

Harris nodded. "Anything you want."

He moved on to the next buffalo. This was a large bull that had dropped not ten feet away and he kicked it gingerly before leaning over it. One of the legs moved slightly and he jammed the knife in at the back of the head, where the skull met the spinal cord, and twisted it. The bull stiffened and its legs quivered.

"Sometimes they lay up on you and get you when you come up. That's what happened to my last partner. Man name of Tinkner. A bull got up on him and stomped him into dirt. I never seen nothing like it. I ran for my rifle and must have shot it six times, but it stayed on the job until you couldn't tell where the dirt stopped and old Tink started. We raked what we could up to bury him. Buried him right there by the bull, up in Kansas. . . ."

Again, all the while he spoke he worked, making the cuts and hooking the team up to the skin to jerk it.

Meanwhile Dirk had taken hump meat from

the cow. It was rich, dark red meat with good fat and his mouth watered while he cut.

"Go ahead, take the tongue too," Harris said from where he was working. "You don't need to leave it for those toffee bastards."

Dirk shook his head. "I don't like tongue. Never have."

Harris nodded. "Just as you like it."

Dirk went to the mule. The flies were on the meat as he carried it and he didn't want them to blow eggs before they could cook it. He untied and opened the feed sack he'd carried food in and while the boy held it open he quickly brushed the flies from the meat and dropped it in the sack. "We eat tonight."

"Ask him," Tilden said.

"Ask him what?"

"About them men. Ask him."

"Oh. I forgot." He wiped his hands on the grass and left the mule to walk back to where Harris was working on a third animal.

"There were four men," he said. "Scavengers—just shit. They hit the boy's family"—he lowered his voice so Tilden wouldn't hear—"killed his ma and pa and carried off his sister. We're hunting them, and I wondered if you'd seen anything?"

Harris looked up from the carcass. He had blood in his hair and beard and on his arms, and Dirk thought how he'd smell come evening. The hunter shook his head. "We ain't seen nothing.

We come down from north following small herds—hoping to hit the big ones—and we ain't seen a single person. Sad about the boy, though. I'd tell you to ask my partners''—his lips pinched at the word—''but they don't know sheep shit from apple butter so it wouldn't do any good.''

''We already asked them, and you're right. They didn't know anything.'' Dirk thanked him and went back to the mule. He swung up and held down a hand for Tilden, who pulled himself up in back of Dirk.

They rode back to the wagon, where the two Englishmen were sitting under the fly tarp in the shade.

''Thank you for the meat,'' Dirk said. They didn't dismount.

''Think nothing of it. Glad we could be of some service to you.'' Clarence Westchester smiled. His upper teeth seemed to stick out and were very white. ''Sorry for the plight of the boy but it's a hard country, what?''

Oh, yes, Dirk thought—it's a hard country. He felt Tilden stiffen in back of him but the boy said nothing and Dirk tipped his hat and they rode off.

Tilden was silent for a time as the mule walked through the grass. It was coming on evening and Dirk was afraid they'd have to make a dry camp. They had some water in two canteens and a flax linen bag Dirk had found at the boy's ranch, but he wanted to wash the meat before they cooked it and there wasn't enough water for that. He could see nothing ahead but grass.

"What were those men?" Tilden asked.

"What do you mean?"

"Why did they talk so funny?"

"Oh. They were English."

"What's that?"

"English?"

"Yeah. What does that mean?"

"They're people from England."

"What's that?"

"England?"

Tilden sighed. "Yes. What's England?"

"It's another country. Like Canada or Mexico."

"Oh. I never heard of it."

Dirk turned to look back at the boy. It was awkward and the barrel of the boy's rifle hit him on the cheek. "You haven't?"

"Nope. Ma and Pa never talked about it and I ain't ever been to school. We had a magazine once that showed all about a city called New York but that's all I've ever seen. Of course I know what Canada and Mexico are."

"Of course," Dirk said, turning back.

"Is it big?"

"What?"

"England. Is it big?"

Dirk shook his head. "No. It's small. An island. It's kind of a small island. Most of it would fit easy into the Oklahoma Territory."

"Damn." The boy snorted. "It must be something—the whole country must be made up of assholes."

"What?"

"Well, hell, if you just happen to meet two of them in the middle of nowhere shooting buffalo and the two of them both happen to be assholes— what are the chances of that? There must be a passel of them back in that place—that England."

Dirk turned in the saddle and looked at the boy. "It's a marvel, how your mind works."

Tilden nodded his head. "That's what my ma always said."

Just then Dirk spied a small stand of willows off to the right of their direction about two miles. It was a thick green spot against the grass, which was beginning to look dry, and he reckoned it for a spring.

"We'll head that way," he said, starting to turn the mule. But the mule saw the spot himself and took up the new direction before Dirk could bring his head around. "There might be water there and we can camp and eat some meat."

DIRK'S eyes were open, but he could not think what had awakened him for a moment.

It was still partially dark, but the eastern sky was graying and the sun would soon be up. He lay awake with his eyes open for a short time, then sat up.

Something had bothered him, awakened him, pulled him out of sleep. He held his breath and listened, looked around, but nothing seemed wrong. They had a comfortable camp on the edge of the willows where as Dirk had hoped they found a fresh spring working out beneath a rock. It was a seeper but he'd dug a hole and it filled with clean, clear water rapidly so they had plenty and to spare for themselves and the mule.

They'd made a small fire with buffalo shit and some dead willow and cooked the meat in strips in its own fat and the two of them had eaten the whole thing—probably seven pounds of meat.

He still had the taste in his mouth.

Nothing was out of the ordinary. The boy slept quietly wrapped in his single blanket, his breath even and slow. Dirk could just see his face in the gray light and Tilden's eyes twitched a bit with some dream.

The ashes were cold, nothing was burning. Sometimes the smell of things burning awakened him. That was from the army too.

Some morning birds were singing, but off and not loud.

The mule was hobbled and stood quietly ten yards away.

Nothing was wrong.

And yet . . .

He shucked his blanket and pulled his boots on. He was dressed still, but he found the Colt and strapped it on, settled the derby on his head and stood.

Goddammit, *something* had awakened him. What was it?

He'd been alive, stayed alive long enough to know that hunches, thoughts, were usually accurate. Once in the army on bivouac he'd snapped awake this way, just this way, and found a sentry asleep and just had time to wake the men and get to his rifle before a reb cavalry unit had hit them. He had not known then either what had awakened him.

He thought back to his sleep, coming awake, trying to remember if there had been anything.

And then he remembered.

Tearing.

There had been some quick tearing sound, loud and short, and as soon as he remembered it, he knew what the sound had been.

There had been gunfire. Far off and quick there had been gunfire, all of it close enough together to make the tearing sound, the shots so close one on another they seemed to be loud tearing cloth.

"Wake up, boy." He reached down to touch Tilden. "Wake up, now."

"What's wrong?" The boy sat up, rubbing his eyes.

"I don't know. I heard shooting and it woke me up. Wait, listen." He held up his hand, held his breath, and the boy did the same.

Faintly, carried on a new morning wind, coming from where they had been, they heard the sound of voices, yelling. They did not last long— less than ten seconds. But they were yelling, and there were some screams.

Dirk watched back east, back toward the hide hunters' wagon, and thought he could detect the flicker of a fire but it was against the dawn sky and he could not be sure.

"What do we do?" Tilden asked. He stood lower and had not seen the light but had heard the sound of voices.

"We leave this spot, now."

"What do you think it is?"

"It might be Indians hitting those hiders, and if it is, they probably know there is a spring here and may come to it for water when they get done there. That's why we leave. We'll circle north and back east and down and see what's going on back there—quiet and easy and low. If it's Indians . . . well, we'll see."

While he was speaking he wrapped his bedroll and saddled the mule, who stood for him quietly.

"Is there something you ain't telling me?" Tilden asked. He was doing the same with his blanket. He used a corner of his shirt to wipe moisture from his rifle barrel.

"No. It's just that it might be what we're looking for. No reason those men to have just kept riding west. They might have stopped somewhere for a time, might have wandered south or north and come back—Christ knows where they went."

He swung up on the mule and held a hand down and Tilden mounted holding his rifle and bedroll. "That might even be them hitting the hiders. Or it all might be nothing—might be they got drunk and are just yelling and popping caps."

But that wasn't what had happened.

They cut back east in the new morning light

and headed south. Dirk found a shallow, dry creek bottom that took spring runoffs and kept the mule moving along it as long as it went in the right direction. It carried them to where he thought they might be half a mile from where the two Englishmen and "their man" had been camped.

He put Tilden on the ground, then dismounted.

"You stay here and hold the mule while I go look."

"I will not." They were whispering and Tilden's voice hissed with anger. "If it's the men, I want a chance to put a ball in them. I have as much right as you to kill them."

Dirk stared at him. He was a kid but yet he wasn't. It was like he was angry because he wasn't going to get candy. "All right. I'll go look, and if it's them, I'll double back and get you before we do anything, all right?"

Finally Tilden agreed and Dirk moved off in the new light of morning.

It was getting brighter with each step and he stayed low and worked south and west. They had lost sight of the flickering of light from fire because they'd been moving down the depression, but now the wind shifted a bit and he caught the smell of smoke and fire and something else he remembered from the war. It was a smell he would never forget, a smell that stuck in his nostrils and gagged him—burned flesh. He'd come on a farm in Pennsylvania and soldiers had burned it with the people in the house and the smell had stayed in his clothes, in his hair and mind for weeks.

He smelled it now.

He had pulled the Colt and held it ready and eased over the edge of a cut bank.

The wagon was about a hundred yards away. It was burning, or had burned for a time, but it hadn't caught well and the fire smoldered.

He could see no people at first. Everything in the wagon was out and strewn around on the ground—it was as if a great hand had grabbed the wagon and shaken it.

He lay for a moment, studying the scene, waiting. Against the back wheel of the wagon there was a shapeless blob he thought to be part of a hide pulled up, but as he watched part of it moved and he realized it was a man.

A burned man.

Still he watched, waited, for a count of fifty. There was nothing he could do for the man anyway. It was hard to tell from this distance that it was even a man.

At last he decided whoever had done this was gone and he stood and walked forward, still slowly, the Colt ready.

It was a man. Or had been a man. He could not tell which Englishman it was at first but knew it was one of them because he found Harris's body off to the side. He had been shot with gunfire and then riddled with arrows so that he looked like a porcupine. Then he'd been cut open and dressed out, his guts pulled out on the grass like he was a hog.

He found Clarence not too far from Harris. Both men had been stripped completely nude and Clarence's parts were cut off and put in the opening where his guts had been pulled out. He was also full of arrows, only he had been alive when they shot him because one of the arrows had gone in his left eye and his hands were still on it as if he had been trying to pull it out.

"Christ."

Dirk whispered it. As much a prayer as anything else. He went to the man at the wagon wheel—by deduction it had to be Harold, the silent Englishman. He was still alive, but just, and would die soon.

He was saying something but there were no lips and damn little tongue left. Dirk was amazed that life was still in him, considering.

But the small sounds came from him and after a time Dirk thought he might be asking for his mother. He had apparently been held over the flames while the wagon was still burning, perhaps tied over them, until he was nearly roasted, then dropped by the wheel where he'd landed in a half sitting position. His burned arms ended in his groin and Dirk could see they had taken his parts as well.

Dirk turned away. Other than using a knife, which he wouldn't do, there was nothing he could offer except to wish the man a speedy death, which he did. As he would have wished for himself in the same circumstances. He would have shot the man except that he did not want to make the sound of gunfire—he did not know how far they had gone. Those who did this.

Indians then, he thought. He walked in a quick circle to find tracks and saw they led off to the northwest. A large group—between seven and twelve riders. He couldn't tell exactly how many.

But enough of them. To kill him and the boy. Plenty of them.

They'd have to leave and make it fast and make it right. If they went the wrong way . . . He let it trail off in his mind.

He turned to go back for the boy, deciding they should best keep going west and maybe a little south, which would carry them off at an angle away from the Indians. He figured they'd gone to the spring, as he'd thought in the first place; he'd just turned and started back when he caught movement out of the corner of his eye.

He dropped to one knee and the Colt came up, the hammer back, when he realized he was aiming at one of the workhorses that had been pulling hides for Harris. He waited, holding his breath, the Colt still on the horse; fear held him, he could smell it on himself.

When nothing else showed he stood again and walked to the horse.

The animal stood quietly, almost passively, and Dirk thought it strange—the other horse in the team was dead, close to the body of Harris—until he saw the blood on the horse's head.

They had shot him then, but the bullet had just capped him and put him down, had not penetrated the skull.

It must have caused great pain. He was still stunned, and Dirk walked up to him and took his halter easily. He had been picketed on a long line so he could graze in the night and Dirk coiled and tugged slightly on the rope, gently to not cause pain, and the horse followed him. It was not a true workhorse but more a wagon horse; a large Morgan breed that could be ridden but was better on a wagon or buggy.

He went back to the depression and was surprised to find Tilden still there with the mule. He'd been certain the boy would not mind him.

"Indians," Dirk said shortly. "All that's left is this horse. . . ."

"You mean they're all dead?"

Dirk hesitated, thinking of the man by the wagon. Then he nodded. "Dead."

Tilden thought a moment, the morning sun lighting his face. "You didn't see any powder or lead, did you?'' He raised a small possibles bag he carried along with his bedroll. "I'm running low on both balls and powder."

Jesus, Dirk thought, the kid's hard. Didn't care a spot for the dead men. Then he remembered he had seen his mother and father killed, had buried them, seen his sister carried off. I'd be hard, too, he thought—hell, I *am* hard. He'd walked away from the burned Englishman like he'd been toast—he had a lot of nerve to think bad of the kid.

"Nothing," he said. "Just the horse and smoke and bodies. We don't have time to look. Near as I can figure they went toward the spring and I'm hoping we'll miss them."

But, he thought. But there might be one of them double back for something. But they might all get into the skull-thud the Englishmen must have had in the wagon and decide to come back and raise a little more hell. But they might cross the mule's tracks at the spring and decide to follow them to see where they led. But. But. But.

He felt great urgency and helped the boy on the Morgan—was pleased to see it stand for the boy and not buck. He hadn't been sure it was broken to ride. But either it was trained or the head injury had mellowed it enough to take a rider.

He started off, pulling the rope tied to the Morgan, and found himself heeling the mule, trying to pick up the speed.

There were too many buts.

A S it happened the first but had been correct.

Apparently two of the Indians had cut the sign and decided to ride off from the rest and follow the tracks back to see where they had gone—probably figuring if anything came of it they didn't want to share it.

They were riding good mounts, two solid cross ponies, and they caught Dirk and Tilden before they were two hours from the burning wagon.

Dirk was just thinking how lucky they'd been. He'd pushed the mule and was gratified to see that the Morgan kept up and stayed docile to the lead rope, and he was just thinking in the morning sun, just thinking how lucky they'd been to get away when Tilden stopped him.

"Somebody's coming," the boy said.

Dirk stopped, listened, could hear nothing for a second, then heard it. Or felt it. The stiff thud of hooves as horses are run on packed earth.

He looked around.

And every goddamned thing was wrong.

There was nothing, no cover for half a mile or a mile in any direction. Flat as a chalkboard. Not a rock bigger than his head. And from the sound of the hooves it was more than one man and they were too close and too fast for Dirk and the boy to get to cover.

So.

This was where it would be, then.

He dismounted and told the boy to do the same. He could see the riders now. Two of them, coming hell-bent and whipping their horses, two small clouds of dust raised as they came.

"We'll only get time to shoot once," he told the boy. "Let them get in close. Really close. Don't worry if they start shooting while they ride. Chances are they won't hit anything."

Tilden said nothing, stood watching the riders come on, fogging their mounts, smelling the kill.

Dirk wrapped the left rein of the mule in his hand, turned the animal sideways, and stood in back of him. He propped his arms over the mule's back and held the Walker in both hands. It had a nub of a sight and he tried to remember where he had held on the riverbank with Pisspot and

Mob—it seemed like years back—when they were shooting. He decided he'd hold on the center of mass.

"Aim at the middle of the biggest part," the sergeants had told them while they watched the gray lines coming at them, yelling and screaming. "You'll hit something." But of course they hadn't been told the Johnnies were aiming at the middle of the biggest part as well—and both sides "hit something."

Four hundred yards now and Dirk thought, They'll curve off. He looked down. Tilden had settled on his butt in the dirt, had both legs up in front of him and was using his knees as a brace. He might as well have been target shooting. He looked small, young, a touch of wind lifted the hair on the back of his neck beneath the brim of the old hat he wore. Looked every inch a kid. But the rifle barrel was steady.

Two hundred yards. They'll curve off now, Dirk thought again. They can't ride right into it. He could see them clearly, see their faces. One of them was wearing a pink shirt. God knows where he'd gotten the material. Both of them had loose, long black hair and rode like they'd been born on a horse. Which might have been true.

At a hundred yards he eared the hammer back on the Walker, felt the cylinder turn. I hope the cap didn't fall off. Hope it isn't wet. Hope the

powder works. Hope my asshole doesn't fall
out. . . .

"Which one do I take?" Tilden said suddenly.

"Right," Dirk said. "I'll take left." He held the
nub sight of the Walker on the left man. They
were coming, he thought, they were riding right
on in like it didn't matter. Like they were bullet-
proof, invisible. Jesus, it was crazy.

Or drunk.

Fifty yards.

And then it was on them. The time.

Dirk squeezed at thirty yards, shooting up at
the rider, aiming at his chest, saw the smoke bellow from the Walker and cover everything, felt-
heard Tilden's rifle next to him.

He thumbed the hammer again, looked for a
target, but the smoke was so thick from both
weapons he saw only blurs.

Two horses went through them—one of them
half leapt over Tilden—and the mule went crazy,
all in the same instant. Shooting the Walker over
his back was a new experience for him and he
reared, jerked to the side, and nearly pulled Dirk
off his feet before he could get unwrapped from
the rein.

He wheeled, ready to shoot, saw the horses,
brought the Colt up.

But it was needless. Both horses were riderless.

He turned back to the front. The smoke
thinned almost at once and he saw that both rid-

ers were down, had both been taken off their mounts cleanly. The one on the right, the man in the pink shirt—Tilden's man—was still and seemed to have been driven into the dirt headfirst. Nothing on him moved and his face was buried.

Dirk's man was watching him. He lay on his side and watched Dirk but did not move. There was a clean hole in the center of his chest and he lay on his side looking at Dirk, then at Tilden, and said something—Dirk did not understand it—and died without moving his arms.

Tilden all this time had been reloading the rifle. Powder from a horn, then a patched ball, carefully rammed down onto the charge, then a percussion cap on the nipple. Reloading calmly. When he was finished—half a minute had passed—he walked up to the dead man in the pink shirt and turned him over.

The ball had taken him in the middle of the throat.

"High," Tilden said. "I held on his chest and shot high. I must have pulled it."

Dirk stared at him. He was calm and quiet, serious. Might as well have been target shooting.

Dirk shook his head. "You're a hard punkin seed, kid."

Tilden looked at him but said nothing, and Dirk turned to the horses.

Neither man had shot as they rode in though

they were armed fairly well. Better than Dirk. He couldn't think what they must have been doing. Both carried breech-loading rifles—.45-70s—and Dirk took the best one for himself. He went through the clothing on the bodies but found nothing in the pockets. Both Indians were dressed in trousers and shirts but wore pouch-sacks tied around their necks.

In the pouches he found cartridges for the rifle. Six in one and nine in the other. He shook them one at a time to make certain the powder was still loose in them and discarded one that seemed to have caked.

"You want to change weapons?" he asked Tilden, pointing at the other rifle.

"I'll stay with this," Tilden said, holding up the muzzle loader. "I know how it shoots." He was still looking down at the dead man and his voice was even, calm, but somehow tight—as if he were trying to control it.

Dirk shrugged. "Just as you like."

He broke the rifle on a rock, clubbing it until the stock broke off, then turned to the Indian horses. Both were ponies and they were grazing calmly not twenty yards away. It was something that amazed him during the war—the horses. The cavalry could charge, screaming and shooting, right into massed cannon and take a full load of grape, get wiped out, and those horses that didn't get hit would often just stop and start calmly grazing on the battlefield, walking carefully between the bodies of the men who had been riding them.

"Help me catch the horses," Dirk said, but it wasn't necessary.

The horses held for him and he walked right up to them and took their reins. Both were wearing bridles and saddles and on the saddles were bedrolls. He worked fast now, took the bedrolls off the saddles and opened them, found little of interest.

"What's the hurry?" Tilden said, noting Dirk's haste.

"We're out of time." He spoke without looking up, scrambling through the goods on the ground. An old tin pot, some coffee—which he set aside— and a small packet of salt. Two dented canteens, which were nearly full of water, and these, too, he kept. The rest was junk or too old to use. "One of two things happened. Either these two came back alone, looking for more fun at the wagon, and saw our tracks—or they followed us all the way from the spring."

"So?"

"Either way the rest of them have a good chance of coming when these two don't come back—for curiosity if nothing else. So they'll find our tracks as well. And they'll probably follow us. We got lucky with these two but that doesn't mean we'll stay lucky. So we've got to move, and we've got to move fast and far. That's so—all right?"

Tilden nodded. "Just asking."

He set to as well and began to help. Dirk decided to keep his mule but he assigned one of the ponies—a good-sized paint—to Tilden and they let the Morgan go. It was too slow and big. The other pony they took as a pack animal and Dirk left the saddle on it and rigged it to carry twin sacks, which he fashioned out of the bedrolls.

"Now we ride," Dirk said. "Let's go."

He mounted the mule and aimed it southwest, not giving the animal its head any longer. Ten minutes he held a canter, dragging the pack pony with Tilden bringing up the rear, then ten minutes at a trot—which jarred his teeth loose—ten minutes at a walk and ten minutes dismounted and leading the animals.

Then again, and again—ten, ten, and ten they called it in the army. Forty miles a day on beans and hay. All day. Except that it would make more than forty miles if they kept it up, could keep it up.

The main ingredient was water. The animals could move well and long without food, or grabbing a rest now and then to take a mouthful of grass—though a few pounds of oats would have helped a great deal. But without water they would go down rapidly and by the end of the first day it would be over.

For now all they could do was keep moving, and hope they found water by night or before.

Ten, ten, and ten.

He drove the mule.

C·H·A·P·T·E·R

☆ ———— *10* ———— ☆

A S it happened they got a bit more water
than Dirk planned on.

They rode all day—Dirk thought they
must have come close on thirty miles by midafternoon—and toward evening they came to some
ridges that stuck up like a hog's back. They still
had not found water and they'd used up most of
what they had in the canteens for the ponies and
mules.

As they moved up the ridges Dirk stopped and
studied their back trail and saw a small plume of
dust not a mile back.

It gave him a start—he could not think how
they could have caught up so fast—until Tilden
shaded his eyes and studied the dust.

"It's the Morgan," Tilden said. "It's following us."

And in a few minutes, as the horse neared, Dirk could see that he was right. The Morgan was not that much slower after all. But still farther back—six, seven miles out on the flats Dirk could see another, larger dust plume, and that was not the Morgan.

"Here they come," he said, almost to himself. "They're doing better than I thought they'd do." He squinted but could not count them. "Can you tell yet how many there are?"

Tilden shaded the sides of his eyes beneath the hat brim, squinted, but finally shook his head. "Nope. It's too far. At least half a dozen, though, by the dust they're making."

"And riding hard to come up on us this way," Dirk mused. "They must have been following the two who came for us pretty close."

He was going to add that they would never outrun them, the way they were coming—he could never get out of a horse or mule what an Indian could. There was an old saying: A white man could ride a horse forty miles and it would drop and he would walk away; an Indian could come along and get the horse up and ride it another hundred and fifty miles and when it went down eat it.

"We'll have to hole up, try to take them," he

said, knowing it was a lie and they would not be able to make it, they would die here.

All of this going through his mind, trying to weigh things, balance things, when a raindrop hit him on the hand.

It had been getting more and more cloudy. Late-summer clouds, high and wet, but he hadn't thought of rain.

In a few moments it was heavier and inside ten minutes it was a downpour, slanting at them, coming with wind, cutting dust and soaking everything.

And wiping out their tracks.

"Now," he said to the boy. "Now we have a chance."

He mounted again, pulled the pony, and signed the boy to follow and turned right. They had been traveling due southwest, moving in a straight line, and Dirk now headed north along the top of the ridge.

He did not do ten and ten any longer. They had to get as much distance as they could while it was raining for their tracks to be covered; travel in a new direction as far as possible if they were to have a chance, and he worried that the rain would not last as many summer rains did not last.

He needn't have worried.

Rather than slacken the rain increased, came down with a roar. They had no slickers and in half an hour everything was soaked through. Dirk

turned to make sure the boy was still with him—
he couldn't see ten rods—and had to smile.

Tilden's hat had lost all shape and was hanging
down around his face like old rags.

He pushed the mule.

They rode into dark and still it rained; grew so
dark he could not see the mule's head and he kept
moving until they damn near fell off a small cliff,
until they had to swim a small stream that had
become a roaring river, until the Indian pack pony
nearly fell on him when the mule stumbled, until
he had to tie a line back to Tilden's pony and finally—near midnight—soaked, reeling, he
thought to hell with it.

If they can move in this, they can have us.

And he stopped.

It was impossible to camp, to get a fire, but they
stopped, and Dirk stumbled around on foot in the
blackness, in the slashing wet blackness until he
came under the side of a rock cliff face. He had
not even seen the cliff.

"We stop here," he said to the boy. He had to
yell to get over the wind and rain. "Hang on to
your horse and come under here."

There was truly no "under" to get inside, but
the slight overhang stopped some of the wind, if
not the rain, which worked in anyway. Dirk tied
the line from the mule to his wrist, had the packhorse tied to the saddle on the mule and took it.

There was nothing else to do, he thought. They

could no longer move without falling off a god damn mountain, they didn't have any real shelter—all they could do was take it.

He felt rather than saw Tilden sit next to him in the mud, and he hunkered and tried to stay warm in his thoughts, if not his body, and a kind of sleep came.

It was not restful, and he could not actually call it sleep, but his eyes closed and his thoughts blurred and something like sleep closed him down.

He dreamt. Strange dreams—more like hallucinations. He thought he saw his mother with a steaming bowl of hot soup. God, it looked good. He wanted to tell her to be careful, to leave the soup by the mule and leave in case the Indians caught up with him, but she left with the soup.

He saw Gettysburg. He had dreamt of Gettysburg many times, of course, as he imagined others who had been there had dreamt of it. But now he saw it more than dreamt it. He saw the bodies again, all of them in fallen lumps and twisted heaps, blown open and bloating. Rows of them. Not even to be used as meat. Just dead men.

Saw it all and mixed it with his mother and the soup and the mules and the Indians and finally, it must have been near three or four in the morning, exhaustion took him and it didn't matter that it was raining or blowing.

He slept.

*   *   *

Tilden awakened him.

The rain had stopped but it was still cloudy. A gray dawn was easing light through the clouds. He couldn't see well yet, but he could make out the mules and ponies—the mule stood looking down on him, seemed to be studying him.

Tilden had moved in next to him in the rain, was snuggled against him, and was having a nightmare.

And why not, Dirk thought. What had come at the kid in the last two, three weeks would make anybody have a nightmare.

Dirk tried to move without awakening Tilden, but it did not work. As soon as he shifted the boy's eyes snapped open.

"I was dreaming of the Indian—the one I shot," he said, looking up at Dirk. He looked small and crumpled. The way a pup looked small when it got wet. Skinny. "I ain't never killed anybody before. In the dream he kept riding at me and I shot and he didn't go down and didn't go down."

Dirk said nothing.

"Is that him coming to haunt me?" Tilden asked. There was real fear in his eyes. "Will he be there always when I sleep?"

And Dirk thought of Gettysburg and the dream he'd had but he lied. "No. It will pass. Don't worry. You're young and it will pass."

He stood. Everything on him hung in wet

folds—it felt like even his skin had become water-logged.

They had loosened saddles in the dark but left them on, held the horses while they sat and dozed, and Dirk now retightened the saddle on the mule and the pack pony.

They were both cranky and he didn't blame them. Standing in the rain all night, not allowed to shake or roll—hell, he was cranky too.

When he threw his leg over the mule it spun once and tried to bite him but came around when he jerked the line.

He could not tell direction in the cloud but headed the mule along the ridge line that he thought took them about straight north. He figured they had come about a half a day south and west when they ran from the Indians and he wanted to get back to the original track and also move off the direction they had been going.

It was like riding in water.

His clothes, the saddle, his derby, the mule—everything was soaked and the boy looked like a drowned pup in back of him.

When he came on to a high part in the ridge after full daylight he stopped and dismounted and studied their back trail.

He could see for miles from their height and there was nothing. Nobody following.

"Can you see anything?" he asked the boy.

Tilden shook his head. "I think we lost them. And the Morgan, too."

"Ahh, yes, I'd forgotten the Morgan." It would follow by smell, he thought, but the rain might have driven that away too, as hard and long as it came down. If it hadn't, they could follow the Morgan until it led them to Dirk and Tilden. If they knew to follow the Morgan. If they could find the Morgan's tracks.

If.

Hell, he thought, there's no sense worrying. All we can do is what we're doing—ride.

He mounted and led the way and they moved half a day north across the ridges. When he judged the sun must be about directly overhead— it had become hot and muggy though still cloudy—he turned left and headed west again.

Through all this he'd remained silent. His clothes were starting to dry somewhat, though very slowly, and when they turned west and headed once more on their original track he turned to Tilden.

"When we get some sun we'll stop and dry our gear."

"*If* we get some sun," Tilden replied. "Can't we back off a little and walk? It seems we must have lost them by now—if we're ever going to. I've got blisters on my blisters. . . ."

He had not complained once but now it was

like a dam had broken and he went on for a time with it.

Dirk let him go. He needed to get it out of his system, and besides, he was right. Dirk was sure they'd lost the Indians. So sure that he had stopped thinking about them and was reexamining what he was doing. Tilden's voice was like a wind, talking of his blisters—Dirk had some of his own—and the rain and the Indians and and and . . .

The truth is, Dirk thought, I'm riding to I don't know where to shoot some men I'm not sure I'll ever find and probably won't best if I *do* find them. So what I'm really doing is riding blisters into my ass to get shot.

Well, he thought, my momma didn't raise a smart boy, did she?

What he ought to do was drop the whole thing. Head west and leave the boy at the first decent ranch he came to. Maybe take a job for a month or two and get some clothes. Maybe settle down.

Sure, he thought. That's it. I should settle down.

Listen to me.

Maybe I should buy a goddamn plow. . . .

He shook his head to clear it. Tilden had gone back to riding in silence and the mule was moving at an even walk. Dirk pulled the Walker out of the holster. He had not had time to reload after shooting the Indian and by now the powder was probably too damp to be used without drying out. But he checked the five unused loads and was surprised to find the nipples dry when he pulled the caps off. He could not be certain without firing but it seemed the loads must be dry as well and he put the gun back in the holster.

The .45-70 was across his lap and he examined it to make sure it was all right. It was a Springfield cavalry carbine, army issue—he wondered if the Indian had taken it off a dead soldier. They were a difficult rifle to use. He much preferred the Sharps or the newer Henry repeating rifles, even the Spencer. The trapdoors on the Springfields had a nasty habit of jamming on the third or fourth shot when the powder built up a bit—they even came with a special tool for unjamming. He thought on how many soldiers in the war were found dead with the unjamming tool in their hands.

Of course he didn't have the tool, or any tools. But he opened the breech and pulled the shell out and saw there was a spot of rust inside the chamber.

They'd have to get some grease and take some time to fix things or they'd rust and rot away.

He slipped the shell back into the rifle and looked ahead. The mule was plodding now and he heard the Indian pony and Tilden's mount doing the same thing in back on him but he kept them moving.

In midafternoon, finally, the sun caught them.
It was like a blessing.

Tilden had not said a word for close on to two
hours and the mule had a stubbornness to its
movement that meant he would stop before too
long and then suddenly the clouds blew open and
it was there.

Hot and bright and lifting them.

"That's enough," Dirk said. "Let's stop and
spread our gear to dry. . . ."

He pulled up and they dismounted. It took
them just a few minutes to picket the horses and
mule with a long rope and spread all their gear on
the low brush around them to dry.

"I was starting to feel like a prune," Dirk said.
"Wrinkles all over."

Tilden was sitting on the ground in his trousers,
his shirt on a branch to dry, working on his rifle
with the corner of a partially dry piece of cloth.
"I've been out in rain but not to where you
couldn't get out of it that way. It takes you down,
doesn't it?"

Dirk wondered if he was talking about the
nightmare and the Indian but he said nothing.

"Do you think it would be all right to sleep?"
Tilden asked. "Or do we have to ride again right
away?"

Dirk rubbed his chin, felt the beard growing
there. He'd shaved once with the old men, using
Pisspot's ivory-handled razor but that had been,

what, close to a week and a half ago? He studied
the back trail, back along the top of the ridges.

"I don't see how they could still be tracking
us," he said. "After that rain. Nobody could track
in that. And we can't just keep driving the animals. And it would be nice to catch some shut-
eye. We'll sleep in turns. You take a few hours
and I'll watch, then I'll . . ."

He turned to Tilden but the boy was already
asleep. He'd been sitting with the rifle in his lap
and he had rolled over to his side and was sleeping
on his hands, the rifle sticking up in the air.

Dirk moved the rifle and Tilden didn't stir.
Then he found a rock, sat with his back to it and
the .45-70 across his knees, and let the sun cook
him until his eyes wouldn't, couldn't stay open
and he was asleep as well.

DIRK lay on his stomach and studied the
buildings.

"Come on, let's get down there," Tilden said. "We ain't going to find nothing up on
this goddamn ridge."

The boy had been swearing more and more, like
he was testing water, and Dirk wished he had a
pa here who could box his ears. They'd ridden
three days after the ridges, moving through grass
country in hot, muggy weather and chiggers so
bad they were both sores all over. It was worst
under their belts and hat bands, around their ankles, but the little bugs had gone other places as
well and Dirk thought he must look like a leper.

Three days of riding in beautiful weather and
no sign of anyone on their back trail and the boy

all the time swearing more and more; three days of eating rabbit and beans and a sage hen the boy had shot with his rifle—or what was left of it. He'd aimed at the head—the fool bird wasn't ten feet away—but hit low and the shock had made a cloud of feathers ten feet across. Three days of riding.

To get on this low rise where he now lay.

Before him was what might pass for a settlement in the Oklahoma Territory. Two buildings stood side by side, low frame buildings with rough board siding, and one outhouse to the rear of them. There were no trees around them, just flat prairie grass. They were weathered and gray and stood out like two carbuncles.

There were chickens—always chickens—moving in the dust in front of the buildings, and a skinny dog lay at the corner.

But no sign of people.

That was why Dirk had stopped. They had seen the buildings for over a mile and there was no smoke from the chimney and no movement; no horses, no cattle, no goats, no sheep. Just chickens.

He was just going to tell Tilden to move to the side and they would go in carefully when the clapboard door on the right building slammed open and an old woman dressed in a red dress came out and threw a basin of water into the dirt. She turned and went back into the building.

"Well, there you have it," Tilden said. "Let's go in—maybe they got some food."

But before they could move the door opened again and the same old woman came out and threw another pan of water in the dirt.

And again.

And again.

"There's something wrong with her," Tilden said. "She ain't working right or something."

Dirk moved back to the base of the mound where he'd left the horses and mule and mounted. "Sometimes when people get old they get to where they do things over and over, forget things. That's all it is. But why isn't there anybody else around?"

They rode up to the buildings, which took five minutes or so, and the old woman came out four more times with water.

On the fourth trip Dirk and Tilden were sitting their mounts near the porch when she came out and she had to turn the pan sideways not to throw water on the mule. She was very old—he thought—eighty or ninety although it was hard to tell. Her dress was filthy and her hair was tied back with a piece of twine but was matted and dirty and she was very thin; critically thin, as if she had not eaten for a time. She had a string tied around her wrist that led back under the screen door into the house.

"Hello," Dirk said. "We were wondering if you could . . ."

But she had turned and gone in again with the pan. Before he could dismount he heard the sound of a kitchen pump working and in a moment she came out with another pan of water that she threw at his feet in the dirt.

This time she started, as if seeing the horses for the first time. She stood, staring at them. Dirk could see that the cord had cut into her wrist and there was a smear of blood around it.

"Hello," Dirk said again.

"Sary," the old woman said. "Sary Gunderson. Sary Gunderson. Sary Gunderson. . . ."

"It's her name," Tilden said. "She's telling us her name."

She looked at him suddenly, nodding. "Sary Gunderson. I'm nine years and four months old. Sary. And I got to clean up or Mom will whip me blue. Got to clean up." And she turned and went back in with the pan and the pump started working again.

"Let's check the other building," Dirk said, turning the mule. "See what's going on. . . ."

He rode to the front of the building and dismounted and went in. It had been a crude trading post. Or at least a storage area of some kind. There were some buffalo skins stacked in the back, salted and dried, and barrels of flour. In front was a board on two barrels that must have been a counter. There were goods scattered all over the place. Bolts of cloth had been pulled down and unrolled and jars of canned goods were broken and thrown about the floor.

In the corner on a feed sack on the floor sat a man.

It was dark in the room and in the bad light the sitting figure gave Dirk such a start that he pulled the Walker, or had it half out, when he realized the figure wasn't moving.

It was a dead man.

And when his eyes got accustomed to the dark and his nose to the smell he could tell that the man had been dead for some time—long enough for the flies. They were around him in droves and rose buzzing when Dirk moved closer to the body, settled again when he moved back.

"What's in here?" Tilden had held the animals and come in after tying them. "What's that in the corner—oh, God."

He ran back outside, leaned against the wall, and threw up.

Dirk studied the room a bit longer. The smell bothered him as well but he had smelled it before, and heard the flies—Christ, the flies at Gettysburg, in the ditches with the bodies they were in clouds—and he wanted to know what had happened.

The man had been shot several times in the chest and had fallen back in the corner on the feed sacks. He was not cut or mutilated—as the hiders had been—so it probably wasn't the Indians.

They've been here, Dirk thought. It's them. It must have been. It had been warm and the body was bloated almost beyond knowing—actually pushing the shirt and pants out tightly—but he guessed that might mean a week in this heat. They were moving slow, then, with the girl. Maybe a week and a half.

He found an empty feed sack and gathered some jars of canned goods. Peaches, and tomatoes, four jars of pickles. He left some jars of meat because he didn't trust canned meat—seen too many men die from it in the army.

When he went back outside Tilden was standing holding the horses and mule again. His face was an off shade of gray.

"That man was about to explode," the boy said. "How could you stay in there?"

Dirk didn't answer. Instead he set the sack aside and went back to the first building, where the old woman was still throwing pans of water out. He stopped outside the door and turned to Tilden. "Picket the animals on a long rope and bring them water in that bucket by the door while I see what can be done here."

Tilden turned to do as he was told—which surprised Dirk because the boy had been getting stiffer with his lip—and Dirk went inside.

She had just dumped a pan of water and was at the pump, over a basin in the kitchen, pumping water into the pan again.

"Sary," Dirk said. "Is there anybody else here?"

"Have to clean up," she said, her back to him, her bony shoulders jerking as she worked the pump. "Have to clean it all up or Ma will whip me blue."

"No, Sary, Ma won't whip you. Ma wants you to sit and talk to me and tell me if there is anybody else here."

That stopped her. She turned away from the pump and sat at the kitchen table. The house was a mess with dirty dishes on the floor, broken and scattered.

Dirk was not sure how to speak to her. "Are you alone here, Sary?"

She stared at her hands on the table. They were still and thin.

"Ma wants you to tell me."

"Only Billy and me are here and Billy's being bad. He's hiding and won't come out."

"Who is Billy?"

"Billy is Ma's grandson."

Her son, he thought, it's her own son—the dead man in the other building. "Anybody else? Is there anybody else here?"

"Sary," she said again, "Sary Gunderson. Sary Gunderson. Sary Gunderson. . . ."

"Did other men come, Sary? Did four other men come? Bad men?"

The old woman looked at him sharply, her eyes wide with fright and suddenly clear.

"Pretty girl," she sang, her voice small and lilting like a child's, "pretty girl a-crying and a-crying—pretty girl with red hair a-crying."

"That's Ellie," Tilden said. He'd come in after taking care of the horses. "That's Ellie. Find out how long since they were here. . . ."

But his arrival in the room seemed to startle the old woman and she became quiet, staring at the tabletop, and Dirk thought again of the bad wind.

We have to bury him. He stood. We have to bury him and then we have to do something about this old woman and I don't know what that can be. . . .

"See if you can't clean her up," he told Tilden. "And make something to eat for her and us. A soup or stew. Do a couple of those chickens." He started for the door.

"Where you goin'?" Tilden asked.

"You don't want in on this one, kid. Just do as I said and I'll be back in a while."

C·H·A·P·T·E·R

12

DIRK sat on the porch and set the plate of food aside. He'd taken two bites of it and was still ravenously hungry but the smell from burying was in his nose and he couldn't eat.

"Ain't you hungry?" Tilden said around a mouthful of stew. He'd plucked two chickens and thrown them in a pot with potatoes, found some salt and pepper, and it smelled and tasted wonderful. Even the old lady, still sitting at the table, had eaten, though weakly.

"I'll eat later."

Tilden nodded. "I know. . . ."

Truth was, Dirk didn't know what in hell they were going to do—or if they could do anything.

One day, he thought—one day I'm riding alone and doing fine, settling down to an evening meal.

Then the hammer drops and now I'm a nanny to a boy and an old woman and I don't know the smallest part of what to do.

The old woman couldn't travel and he couldn't stay. There it was. And Tilden wasn't about to stay with the old lady.

"When do we leave?" Tilden said as if reading his thoughts. The late-afternoon sun was hot on them and Dirk leaned back against the wall. His butt had softened during the time at Pisspot and Mob's place and was just now getting saddle-hard again.

"The stock needs rest," he said, thinking. "It won't hurt to lay up a day. Maybe we can find some grain for them."

"But we're closer. You heard the old lady. They were here and they've still got Ellie. We keep going now and we might get on them in a few days or a week. We lay around a week and we'll lose them sure."

Dirk studied the boy. "What about the old lady?"

"What about her?"

"You just want to leave her?"

Tilden thought on it.

"She can't ride," Dirk prompted. "And if we leave she won't last long. She was moving poorly when we came."

"You ain't leaving me." Tilden's jaw tightened. "Don't even think on that a little bit, by God."

Dirk shook his head. "To be straight honest I don't know *what* to do."

Tilden shook his head. "You ain't leaving me," he repeated. He took another mouthful of the chicken stew.

Dirk stood and went into the kitchen and found the old woman standing at the pump once again. But this time there was purpose to her. She pumped water into the pan and put it on the stove to heat, moving slowly. The twine was gone from her wrist and when she looked at Dirk her eyes were bright, had lost the nonthinking dullness.

"Who are you?" she asked.

Dirk was startled. "What?"

"I said, 'Who are you?'" She stacked some dishes near the stand for the dishpan. "What people are you?"

"I'm Duncan Prine, ma'am," Dirk said. "People call me Dirk. And the boy is Tilden Holmes."

"Are you after those men?"

"Ma'am?" He could not believe such a change could take place. She was as clear as a bell. But he did not know for certain how much she knew—did not know if she knew the man in the store was dead. Her son. And he was afraid to startle her.

"Those four men who were here—are you after them?"

He decided to tell the truth. "Yes, ma'am."

"Are you going to kill them?"

"Ma'am?" He felt stupid, trying to keep up with her and figure out how she could have changed so much.

She raised a hand and pointed a thin, frail finger at him; an old, old finger. "Look here, young man, I'm going to die soon and before I go I want to know these things are being done. Now you tell me, are you going to kill those four men who were here?"

Dirk sighed. "If it happens that way, then I guess I will, yes."

"Can you?"

He waited.

"Can you kill them? Are you strong enough?"

"I'm not sure how you mean it. . . ."

"Do you have the will?"

Oh, Dirk thought. The will. He remembered the man pointing the pistol at his head and pulling the trigger, the flash as he thought his life was ending, the flash and then the nothingness. Do I have the will? "Yes, ma'am."

She smiled. All her teeth were gone and the smile was almost a mask. "Good. You find them and you kill them and you'll have one old woman's blessings."

"Was there a girl with them?" Tilden had come into the kitchen during the conversation. "A red-headed girl?"

"Sad thing," Sary said. "She was a sad thing. Sat in the corner and moped and cried."

"That's her," Tilden said. "That's Ellie—they've still got her with them."

"Bury me with the boy," the old woman said suddenly, looking at Dirk.

"Ma'am?" He felt foolish—just saying it again and again. Ma'am? "What did you say?"

"I'm going to make my deathing place now and I want you to bury me with the boy, with Billy. You buried him, didn't you?"

Then she knew. "Yes, we did."

"Bury me next to him. It's a great sadness, having your children die before you, a great sadness, and I'm sick of it, sick of it, sick of it. . . ."

She moved slowly, seeming to creak with the steps, out of the kitchen into a back room that Dirk knew was the bedroom, and he wondered if she could do that. Could she just go and die?

Tilden hadn't moved. "How come she's so different?"

Dirk shook his head. "I don't know. It just came." I should have asked her more, he thought. I should have asked when they were here. He went to the bedroom door and looked in.

The room was darkened with no windows and the bed messed, furniture tipped over. The old lady was already on the bed, lying on her back with her hands folded on her breast.

"Sary?"

She did not move and he could not see well enough to tell if her chest was rising with the breathing. He walked to the side of the bed. "Sary?"

"Yes." A whisper, quiet, soft—almost a little girl's voice.

"How long ago were the men here?"

She didn't answer for a long time, then again it was a whisper. "I don't know. I can't tell time anymore. There just isn't any—isn't any time for me, for me, for me. . . ."

And she died.

It was that quiet. A last breath went out of her and no new one came back in and she took death gently while Dirk stood next to the bed waiting for an answer; took it clean and simple between breaths.

They did as she wished, buried her next to the man they had found in the store, and Dirk tried to find some words but didn't know any except the Lord's Prayer. So he and Tilden did that but the boy was fidgeting to go—couldn't stand for more than a few seconds with wiggling—and Dirk had to make him stay and put rocks over the dirt in the shallow graves to keep the coyotes out.

But at last they were done and though it was almost dark Dirk allowed the boy's restlessness to infect him and they saddled the horses and mule, loaded food and some other goods they found in the storage building—another box of twenty .45-70 shells—and rode away in the dark.

West.

Always west.

C·H·A·P·T·E·R

THEY had a moon. Dirk let the mule head west in the moonlight and thought how stupid it was to travel at night. But they had a good moon, full and covering the prairie grass with soft, white light so at least they could see where they were going, and it wasn't somehow possible to stay a night at the settlement after they buried the old woman.

The thought of bad wind came back again to him. These men. Just blowing like a bad wind, like a storm across the land. A death storm.

In back of him Tilden—silent and lost in his own thoughts, or asleep, Dirk thought—plodded along, the pony easily tracing the mule.

We'll just ride awhile, Dirk thought—get away from the bodies—then we'll pull up and make a dry camp and catch some sleep. No sense in riding all night.

They had left in a hurry, almost running, and at the time Dirk wasn't sure if they were running from something or running to something—trying to catch up to the men.

He thought suddenly of Ellie, tried to picture her in his eye. Red hair, freckles, dirty, used . . . badly used by now. They would be at her. What must it be like—to be a woman and be used that way? He'd seen it in the war. Saw a man hanged for it, hanged for a farm girl in a caved-in basement, and felt good when the son of a bitch danced on the rope. Anybody who'd do that, he thought, a girl like that—anybody who'd do that should get a slow drop.

Ellie. She sounded older than the girl in the war, who'd been just twelve or so. A young woman, Ellie. And maybe tough, from what Tilden said. But how much longer could she last?

They'd tire of her, these men, tire of her, and then one of them would shoot her or stick her or choke her or . . . they didn't care. They didn't have it in them to care.

The mule shied gently at a snake. Dirk could just see it move in the grass. Then they were past and he turned to see the Indian pack pony and Tilden's pony as well move sideways around the snake in the moonlight.

Good stock was hard to beat, he thought. He'd

had good and bad horses and a bad horse could ruin your whole day.

What were they going to do when they caught up to these men?

He shook his head. He was starting to plan things that were out ahead too far. Hell, he thought, remembering the two Englishmen and the hider, the Indians chasing them. Next time we might not have the rain and that will be the end of us. And I'm planning.

He dozed.

His eyes closed and he dozed and finally fell almost sound asleep and did not awaken until he sensed that the mule had stopped.

He opened his eyes to see that they were on the edge of a shallow, wide depression, almost a valley. It went below and away in the moonlight like a great bowl and he could see dark blobs moving in it that he realized were small herds of buffalo. Ten and twenty in each, moving in the moonlight.

"Oh." Tilden's voice came next to him as the boy's pony pulled alongside. "Ain't it pretty?"

Dirk nodded without saying anything. He thought they should stop here, camp before they started down the wall of the basin that might prove tricky in the moonlight, but he'd spotted something on the other side of the bowl and he watched for it again.

There.

A flicker of light. It must be close to two miles across the valley and the light was on the other side but even so it must be small. A small campfire.

"I see a light," Tilden said, almost at the same instant. "Over on the other side. . . ."

"I saw it."

"Well, let's go. What if it's them?" Tilden heeled his pony and it jerked but held back at the thought of going over the edge of the rim down into the basin. "Goddammit, let's go." Tilden sawed the pony's head around.

"Take it easy," Dirk said. "You'll bust a leg in the dark. We'll have to dismount and lead them down."

He did so, tying the packhorse's line to the mule's saddle horn and starting down the incline. It was three hundred feet and more of a sharp drop, but it went fast because he almost fell ahead of the mule and the mule dragged the pony.

Even in the dark it worked well enough and at the bottom he mounted and heard Tilden do the same. He'd lost the fire as they came down, lost visibility, but he'd marked a star to follow and they started moving across the shallow valley through the small buffalo herds.

He was almost certain it wasn't the men. The nearest they could be would be a week ahead of Dirk and the boy and it wasn't likely they would sit by a fire for a week. They didn't move fast, but they seemed to keep moving, seemed to have a purpose.

But it had to be checked out. Maybe they had swung north and back and used up a couple of days. . . .

Hell, he thought, we'll probably never see them again. They could have gone anywhere.

They covered half the distance across the basin. He still could not see the fire, but he thought he sensed a glow where it had been. When he judged they were still a half a mile from it, he stopped and dismounted and started walking, leading the mule. Tilden moved the same in back of him.

When he was a quarter mile from the fire he saw it flickering again and he left the mule with Tilden and walked forward alone. He held the .45-70 ready and the Colt on his hip and when he was still a hundred yards from the fire he stopped and squatted and waited, studying.

It was a small fire. At first he couldn't see anything other than the flames, then he could make out figures. There were two horses tied in some willows not far off and they knew he was there, were watching him with their ears raised, but had not made a sound yet.

There was what looked like a huge bed by the fire that he thought might contain one or two people, but there was such a jumble of blankets he couldn't tell for sure and he decided to move a bit closer.

He eased up but before he could move a blanket was thrown back from the pile and a small Indian boy—five or six years old—went off to the side of the campsite to pee. When he was finished he went back to the blanket and burrowed in, like a puppy looking for a nipple.

Then another child came out, and still another. . . .

"What is it?"

Tilden had crept up in back of him and whispered in his ear and Dirk jumped.

"It's a family of Indians," Dirk said. "Probably following all these buffalo. Let's go back and work around them."

He turned to leave but his movement triggered a response in the Indian ponies and they snorted and stamped and the mule answered. Instantly the blankets were thrown back and a man emerged, running to the side. As he'd come out of the bed he scooped up a rifle and while he was still moving to the right a woman scrambled from the bed with three children and started running to the left, running to hide with the children, and Dirk thought, No, this is going all wrong.

In part of a second it would go too far, he knew, and if the man shot it would be beyond control. He'd have to shoot back.

He laid the rifle down and stood up. "No. Friends. Don't. Don't . . . Tilden, lay your gun down."

"Are you crazy?"

"Now, goddammit. Put it down."

Tilden did as he was told.

And still, for that time it took to suck in half a breath, still it was tight. The man had dropped to one knee and brought the rifle up and Dirk felt his stomach knot up.

But it held. It all held. Dirk spread his arms and walked forward. He smiled. "Come with me," he said back to the boy. "Put your gun down and come forward into the light."

Still it could have gone either way. But after a moment more of hesitation Tilden did as he was told.

And still the man kneeled, watching them walk forward.

"Dirk. I'm Dirk and this is Tilden," Dirk said, low and even. "We're just riding by—do you speak English?"

"Some," the man said suddenly, cutting the word at the end. "From a Quaker I got English. In a school. Are there more of you?"

"No. Just two."

"Why did you not shoot?"

"We mean you no harm. We saw your fire from the rim up there and thought it might be someone else. We are looking for four men. . . ."

"And a woman?" The Indian was still kneeling, the rifle still on Dirk, but the tension had gone out of the situation and he now stood, lowered the rifle. Dirk could see that it was an old flint-lock—probably older than both of them combined.

"Yes. There was a woman. With red hair and freckles. . . ."

"That I can't say. I saw their tracks and the woman got off to go in the bushes so I knew it was a woman. She had been eating much meat and some berries."

"How long ago?" Tilden asked from the rear.

"I'm not sure." He turned and said something in Indian to the darkness across the fire and a woman came out with three small boys. She was fat and had a round face, as did all the boys, shining in the light, and she said something to the man sharply and he laughed.

"She does not trust you. Isn't that strange—that she doesn't trust a white man?" His voice joked but there was an edge to it. "She does not speak white talk because she did not know a Quaker. She says it was four days ago that we saw the tracks and then they might have been one or two days old. I wasn't sure."

Four days, Dirk thought, and maybe six. They might be only six days ahead.

Only.

But if they're riding slow and we push it that might be the same as only two days.

Only.

Tilden had been figuring as well. "We could catch them in three days. Maybe two."

"If . . ." Dirk let it hang. There were so many maybes it didn't seem possible to predict. He faced the Indian again. "We are sorry to cause you trouble."

"You did nothing but awaken us. Would you eat with us? I have much buffalo. . . ."

Dirk was going to say no but Tilden chirped up in back of him. "I'm hungry."

"That's a surprise."

"Come in by the fire," the man said. "And bring your hungry boy in as well."

"I'm not his boy," Tilden said, but followed Dirk in to sit by the fire. The man threw more wood on the flames, which by now had gone down almost to embers, and in a moment there were new flames and more light.

Dirk could see that the man was older than he first thought, much older than the woman who now came in with the three boys and stood in back of him. He might have been fifty, although it was hard to tell because his face was weathered and there was a large scar that went from his upper left forehead down across his right eye and cheek. It gave his face a drooping look, a sadness that wasn't in his eyes.

"There is meat in the pot. Eat. Eat."

But Dirk was looking at one of the boys. He was

about seven and had red hair and freckles and white skin.

"He's white," Tilden whispered, sitting next to Dirk, but the old man heard.

"Not as you think." The old man shook his head. "She is the mother. She is my wife but before me there were some white men who came to the village when she was younger and one of them gave her father much whiskey and the boy came from that time. He is a good boy but his skin cooks and bubbles in the sun."

"We did not mean to look where it's none of our business," Dirk said, throwing a sharp look at Tilden. "Sometimes his mouth goes before he thinks."

"It is because he is young."

"Probably."

All this time the woman had spent taking the pot off the fire and opening the top and the smells that came out made Dirk's mouth water while he spoke. He held back until the children and old man and woman had taken pieces of meat out and then reached in and pulled out a chunk of buffalo meat. There was something else to it, some smell, and he realized it was sage; she must have put sage in the pot with the meat.

A little thing like that, he thought, and it made the meat taste completely different. Better. He ate it though it was so hot it burned his tongue and saw Tilden reach for another piece and shook his head. Tilden's hand came back empty.

The woman had found a blackened coffeepot in a pack on a travois and she poured water from a canteen and broke coffee beans with a rock to make coffee.

It was still dark and Dirk stood. "We'll be moving on. We did not mean to keep you up. . . ."

The Indian laughed. "You did not. It is time to get up. We want to be out of this big dish by hard light. The hunting is good here but sometimes the Comanches come up from that place where the color is and they don't care who they kill."

Comanches, Dirk thought—that was who hit the hiders. We must be north of the Staked Plains. It was lucky the rain had come. He had never seen them, dealt with them before, but had heard about them. In a grayback saloon in Arkansas a drunk was going on about them, about how they hit a homestead and he'd come by later. "They was beating babies with babies," the drunk said, and Dirk would have dismissed it except that there was such fear in the drunk's eyes that he knew the horror was real.

Dirk went back to where they'd tied the mule and horses and the Indian followed.

"The coffee will be good. My woman makes the best coffee."

Dirk shook his head. "No. We'll be going.

When you saw those tracks which way were they going?"

"Tracks?"

"Of the four men. And the woman."

"Oh. They were headed that way." He pointed to the west. "Toward the fort."

"Which fort?"

"Oh, Bent's Fort is over that way." He shrugged. "I do not like that place. There is too much drinking there. But that is probably where they are going."

"How far is it?" Dirk asked.

"Five or ten days, maybe. With your horses maybe seven days, maybe less."

Dirk thanked him and mounted, started riding west away from the fire. Over his shoulder he could sense the light eastern sky bringing dawn. He heard Tilden catch up.

Bent's Fort.

He'd heard about it back in Missouri and Arkansas. Everybody talked about it. It was where you got on the trail down to Santa Fe. The last place God made, they called it.

"What's this fort?" Tilden asked. "What's it like?"

Dirk shrugged. "I don't know. I've never been there."

"But you know about it."

"Yes. I know about it. It's a trading post that calls itself a fort, from what I hear. I guess this man named Bent stopped there and started it up to trade with the mountain men for furs."

"Mountain men." Dirk could hear it in his voice. Awe. He might not know what England was, but he'd heard of mountain men. "Will there be some there?"

Dirk shrugged again. "I don't know. Maybe. They probably come in during the summer and bring pelts to sell. . . ."

"I've always wanted to meet one." Tilden scratched a chigger bite. "Pa talked about 'em. Kit Carson and Jim Bridger. Pa would sit and talk about 'em for hours."

"Well, maybe you'll get your chance," Dirk said. "Because that's where we're going. . . ."

He kneed the mule into a faster pace. The Indian had been right. It wasn't comfortable in the valley when there might be Comanches.

C·H·A·P·T·E·R

B ENT'S Fort didn't seem so much a fort as
it did a madhouse.

They rode for six more days without
seeing a single soul. Twice they saw buffalo and
the second time Dirk dropped one with the .45-
70 to make meat and they ate like lords, sitting
next to a daylight fire and eating hump meat and
fat until they were bloated and greasy with it.

"It's good meat," Tilden said when they had
finished. "Better than any. Better than deer."

And Dirk had to agree with him. It was even
better than good beef. The fire gave it a smoky
taste and it was hard to stop eating even when
they were full. They'd lain by the fire picking at
it a whole afternoon and then slept like the dead

until just before dawn the next day, which turned out to be the last before they hit the fort.

They'd ridden through drier and drier country, the grass growing fall dead and brittle though it was still only early August. Had it not been for a day spent in thunderstorms that ripped around them like the furies and made Dirk pull Tilden and all the stock into a low gully to ride it out, it would have been like a desert. The soil became sandy until the animal's hooves were sinking into it, and just when Dirk was thinking they had missed the fort completely they ran into a trail of wagon ruts.

They came from the east and north and were so deep they looked like cuts across the land. Tilden dismounted and put his hand down to the bottom of a rut and it came up to his elbow.

"It's the Sante Fe Trail," Dirk said. "Comes down from Kansas somewhere and to this fort. We're on the right track. . . ."

And the next day they'd come to the fort. Except that it wasn't a fort.

"I saw a picture of a fort on a calendar once," Tilden said as they rode toward the settlement. "And this sure ain't how it looked."

Dirk agreed.

A series of low buildings seemed to squat in the middle of nowhere and it was hard to see even the buildings for the ramshackle tents and cloth lean-tos that surrounded it. It was like a cross between an Indian village and a fur trappers' rendezvous and there had to be hundreds of men, women, kids, and dogs running all over the place.

Dogs.

Packs of them, Dirk thought, he'd never seen so many dogs. They came tearing at Tilden and Dirk like ravening wolves, startling even the mule into crow-hopping and skittering to get away from them.

"Get down!" Tilden yelled, clubbing with his rifle, but it was impossible to control them and Dirk finally dismounted and started kicking. When he'd landed a few solid hits and produced screams of pain the rest of the dogs backed off.

"Why would anybody want to come here?" Tilden said as they walked and led their mounts toward the center of the mob where the buildings seemed to indicate authority. "It smells like an outhouse."

"I don't know, but we aren't staying." The boy was right, he thought, and for good cause. There were no visible toilets and people apparently just walked out on the prairie and dropped. Dogs fought over what they could get, but what they missed and their own leavings along with the manure from literally hundreds of horses in small herds around the settlement made for thick air. "We'll see what we can see and get out."

Everybody seemed either drunk, getting drunk, close to getting drunk, or coming off a drunk.

Trappers who smelled worse than the surrounding air staggered around with jugs and squaws looking for a place to drop and they didn't much seem to care where it was, judging by Tilden's eyes.

"Look at that," he said, pointing with the end of his rifle beneath a tarp that barely covered a couple. "Just like dogs. . . ."

Dirk kept moving until they were at the buildings where one of them was apparently a store or trading post.

He left Tilden outside holding the stock and went inside where it was stone dark except for a slot of light that came through the door and one broken window.

Inside he moved sideways and let his eyes grow accustomed to the lack of light and when he could see he found a mob of men four deep trying to get to a counter where a clerk—if he could be called that—was dispensing goods. Or trying to.

The clerk was a short, squat man with powerful shoulders and a new Army Colt .45 on his waist, the holster held with a rope. He was cue-ball bald and was completely ignoring most of the men, who held out beaver or wolf pelts for him to see.

He would focus his attention on one man, finger his pelts, blow the hair backward to see down into the fur, and make an offer that was nearly impossible to hear in the noise of all the men pushing and clamoring. There would be nods from the bewhiskered mountain man, or a shake of his head, a jug would come out from beneath the counter, supplies—powder, lead, flour, cartridges—would be brought from the back by another worker, and the clerk would turn to the next man.

I don't have a chance of getting close to the man, Dirk thought. He was about to turn and leave when a man next to him leaned over and smelled him.

"You don't smell like a trapper," he said. He was dressed in rough-spun trousers and an open shirt and the shirt was so stiff with dried blood it was like iron, "or a hider."

"I'm looking for some information," Dirk said. "About some men I need to find." He briefly described what he remembered, the fact that they might be with a woman but not why he was looking for them. "I don't have anything to trade or buy with."

"I just come in with a load of buffalo hides yesterday and I haven't seen them, but you can follow me and I'll show you where to go."

"You'll lose your place in line," Dirk protested.

"Ahh, hell, it don't mean nothing. The line will be here tomorrow, or tonight, for that matter. And I know they're going to screw me on my hides—why should I hurry it?"

He went out the door and Dirk followed him

around to the side of the building where there was another small door.

"Just go in there and you'll miss the herd out front. I saw other men going in and out here. They might be able to help you."

"Thanks," Dirk said.

"No problem." The man held out his hand. "Harris. Bill Harris, but my friends call me Skinner. . . ."

"We met a Harris out in Kansas, doing hides," Dirk said.

"Short coupled man with tight shoulders?" Harris asked. "Answers to the name of Dick?"

Dirk nodded.

"That's my brother. Last I heard he was going off with some Englishmen who were going to stake him—how was he doing?"

Dirk hesitated, remembered Harris's body on the ground, decided to tell the truth. "He was dead. Indians got him and the Englishmen. I think Comanches but I'm not sure."

"Ahh, damn." He seemed to sag. "We were never close but Ma always favored him when we were buttons and she'll take it hard. Did he go fast?"

Dirk lied. "I think so. We weren't there when it happened. . . ." He trailed off. There was no sense in covering details—like the fact that the man's brother was unburied.

Harris walked away shaking his head, dazed,

and Dirk started after him but decided to let him go. There was nothing he could do or say that would help the man.

He opened the door and stepped inside.

It was a storeroom in back of the main part of the trading post out front. In the center was a rough table where a man sat doing figures as the worker came in and went out with blankets and a small keg of powder. The man at the table wrote it down carefully on a sheet of paper, his tongue sticking out the side of his mouth in the concentration. Next to the paper was a book and in the light through an oiled paper window Dirk could see that it was a Bible.

"Trading all takes place up front," he said to Dirk, pointing to the door. "Nobody is allowed back here."

"I'm not here to trade," Dirk said, then explained why he was at the fort. He told it quickly; told about the boy out front and that his sister might be with them, although he truthfully thought they would have tired of her and killed her by now.

"You mean these men ill?" The man at the table was heavy, leaning toward fat, and had a beard twisted off to the sides and greased.

"I mean to get back what's mine," Dirk said. "And the girl, if she's still with them."

"You think they'll just let you come and do that?"

Dirk shrugged. "I guess not. That doesn't matter."

"They'll try to kill you."

"Maybe."

"And you'll have to do ill to them if that happens."

Again Dirk shrugged. "If that's the way it goes, that's the way it goes."

The man put his hand on the Bible next to his tally sheets. "In the Book it says it's wrong to do ill to others."

Dirk nodded. "It also says an eye for an eye and a tooth for a tooth."

"True." He stopped and entered some figures as the man came in from the front and took out another armload of goods. "That's what's so good about the Book—it balances everything out. Would one of these men be named Shaver and would he be limping?"

It came so fast that it surprised Dirk. "What?"

"Would one of them be limping and be named Shaver?"

Dirk nodded. "From a bullet I put in him. The night they tried to kill me." Again he had a mental image of the man smiling at him, pulling the trigger on him, the flash in his face, and then nothing. That was death. That's how it came. He shuddered. "Were they here?"

Parker nodded. "He was, at any rate. I didn't see the rest or the girl you speak of, but he was here. The others might have camped out a ways, but he came and bought some goods—just a minute, I'll tell you.'' He looked back through the stack of tally papers on the table, going down the columns with a stubby finger. "Ahh, here it is. He bought twenty pounds of beans, eight pounds of flour, six of coffee, one pound of salt, and five pounds of sugar. Paid in gold. A double gold eagle.''

Dirk waited patiently and when nothing further came he prodded. "How long ago? When was he here?''

Parker thought, frowning, then snapped his fingers and smiled and consulted the tally sheet again. "Three days ago, exact. I date each entry. It was a slow day and my clerk up front had the bloody flux or I wouldn't have been at the counter when he came in and we wouldn't know all this.''

"He didn't happen to say where he was going, did he?''

"You don't want much, do you? Must have been a hundred men came through—it would be impossible to remember . . . wait a minute . . . he asked about early snow on Laveta Pass. I remember now.''

"What's that, Laveta Pass?''

"It's the pass through the mountains you got to take to get over to Fort Garland and down to Taos. I told him there was no snow and he left.''

"How far is it to Taos?" Dirk asked.

Parker rubbed his cheek through his beard, thinking. "Between a week and two weeks, depending on weather and your mount."

"And now," Dirk said, "one more thing. I've got the boy with me and it don't seem right, taking him. . . ."

Parker nodded. "This is a dangerous thing you do, and possibly an evil one that could corrupt the youth."

Dirk thought of Tilden for a moment, wasn't sure you *could* corrupt him, but nodded. "What I was thinking was that I could leave him here and pick him up on the way back after I get his sister." Or, he thought, just leave him here, if the sister is dead, which he thought would be the case, but he didn't say it.

"An admirable thought. I'll be glad to have the boy as an apprentice, if that's what you wish. Is he strong?"

Dirk nodded. "And tough. Really tough. And smart. He learns fast."

"Bring the boy in and we'll talk it over."

"Ummm . . . it might be better if I just told him and left. He isn't going to be really partial to the idea." It'll be about like trying to hold a badger, he thought. "I'll also need some supplies and I don't have any money. But I'll pay you when I get some, send it back."

Here Parker hesitated, the trader instinct for

profit too strong to be let down easily. "By your own admission you're going after four men who came near to killing you once already. What makes you think you'll be able to pay me later?"

"If I can," Dirk added. "Then too you'll get work out of the boy."

That brightened Parker's face. "There is that. What will you need?"

"Do you have any new Army Colt .45s?"

Parker nodded. "A crate left, but they go fast. I don't favor them myself because you can't tailor your loads like you can with a cap and ball. But they are handy."

And fast, Dirk thought. "And shells?"

Parker nodded.

"Two boxes. And I'll need a little coffee, and salt, and"—he remembered the rain—"a slicker and five pounds of coffee and a sack of belly beans. That should do it."

Parker was working in the tally sheet again, writing it all down. He stood and went to several piles of goods and bins and used old feed sacks cut in half and resewn for the coffee and beans. From a box he brought out a greased Colt, which he put on the table, and from another wooden box two boxes of shells, fifty in each.

When he had everything on the table, a yellow slicker on top, Dirk stood, bundled everything in his arms, and started for the door. "I'll bring the boy in."

Parker nodded. "Whatever works best."

Rope, Dirk thought—that's about the only way the boy will stay. Tied down. But he went outside and decided as he walked that the only way he would get Tilden to stay would be to use the time-honored method adults had always used with young people.

He would lie to the boy.

C·H·A·P·T·E·R

☆ —— 15 —— ☆

D IRK eased into the saddle. He'd rested the mule only four hours and didn't expect to have it blow up on him, but Parker had thrown in twenty pounds of oats and he'd fed the mule and packhorse half a pound each and oats had a way of turning to gunpowder in mules.

But the mule held. He'd made a dry, cold camp, not wishing to make a light that anybody could see. Hell, he thought, not anybody—the boy. He didn't want the boy to see it if he got away from Parker and came.

Truth was he missed the boy. He'd gotten kind of used to Tilden and found himself looking back every once in a while, expecting somebody to say something to him. And he wasn't that fond of leaving the boy with Parker, as far as that went.

Parker was just looking for a navvy—someone to work for him.

But where Dirk was going, what he was going to do when he got there, wasn't a good place or thing to do with the boy.

Of course, he thought, remembering the hiders and the Comanches, it hasn't been all that smooth up to now, come to think of it.

Strangely, the boy had taken it fairly well. He'd argued for a time, and when it became apparent that Dirk wasn't going to let him come, at last he had shrugged and said: "You're coming back with Ellie when you get her?"

And Dirk had nodded and assured him that he would bring the boy's sister back—knowing in his thoughts that Ellie was dead and that he probably wouldn't be coming back.

And he'd spent the night camped nearby, ridden out of Bent's Fort just before dawn and that, he'd thought, was that.

Now he'd spent most of the day riding, stopping to rest the mule and packhorse for four hours in the hot afternoon. It was evening but there were still several hours before dark and he moved the mule west, aimed at the mountains.

"Look for something looks kind of like the rear sight on a rifle," Parker had told him by way of directions. "That's Laveta Pass. But you won't see that for three days. Just ride west and north a bit and follow the trail—hell, that's where everybody goes."

He pushed the mule a bit and was surprised to see that he took it. At first when he'd started riding the mule he'd missed his bay. He'd spent some time on the bay and it understood him and he knew the animal. But the mule was working well for him now, moving to his knees, and when the evening sun started warming his face he let the mule have its head and fell asleep in the saddle.

Not deep sleep, but sound enough so he forgot where he was, dreamt about his mother, and when his eyes snapped open the mule had stopped and he didn't know how long it had been stopped.

"This won't work," he said aloud to the mule. "Even if we catch them it won't do any good to run in on them in the dark."

It wasn't pitch-dark yet, but getting hard to see, and he stopped in a small gully and made a camp. It took him a few minutes to picket the mule and horse, set up his bedroll, and get a fire going, and he was just making coffee when he heard the Indian pony snort.

An answering whuffle came from down the gully.

Dirk eased the new Colt out of his holster and moved off into the brush away from the fire. He didn't cock it, but held it in front at eye level with his thumb on the hammer, both hands holding the revolver ready, aimed at the sound.

There was no movement for a moment, then more sounds from the Indian horse and answering sounds and Tilden rode into the light.

"Where in hell are you?" he said, sitting on his own Indian horse. The pony was lathered and foamed and weaving a bit but still holding up for him. "I rode hard to catch you and you hide on me. . . ."

Dirk stepped out of the brush and holstered the Colt.

"You don't look surprised to see me," Tilden said, dismounting.

"I'm not."

"You don't look glad, either."

"That's the same—I'm not. You should have stayed with Parker."

Tilden looked up at him. The light from the fire made his face look like a quizzical clown—a circus dwarf. Not a boy but a little man. He was dirty, thick with it, and streaked where his sweat had cut the dirt into mud. "All that son of a bitch wanted was a workhorse. . . ."

"Still. You'd have been safe and he'd have fed you, given you a roof."

"I've got a roof. I've got a whole ranch. You forget that?"

Dirk looked at the boy. Something had changed in him. Most of the boy was gone. And just a week, no, two of them—the boy was gone. "Yes. I guess I did forget at that."

"You cook beans yet?" Tilden was taking the saddle from the pony.

"Not yet. I just got here."

"I brought extra. . . ." He untied a bundle from the back of his saddle and pulled out a ham. "Took it off of Parker. He won't miss it. He's richer than God, that Parker."

Dirk gave him the sack of oats for his mount and took the ham. It was crusted with salt and dried honey. Just looking at it made his mouth water. He cut slabs from it and put them in a pan to fry. "We'll skip the beans tonight and just have ham and coffee."

Tilden was silent as he came in to the fire and sat down and remained silent while they cooked and ate and drank coffee. Finally Dirk broke the silence.

"How did you find me?"

Tilden shrugged. "You're using that Indian pony for a packhorse. I had the other Indian pony and I remembered that Morgan trying to follow us. I just let the pony have its head after I got away from the fort and he followed you. . . ."

Dirk smiled. "You have any trouble leaving the fort?"

Tilden shrugged. "That Parker, he tried to keep me in a room—even locked me in. But they left a window open and I got out and found my horse.''

"It was wrong—for me to leave you there. Dead wrong.''

"Yes. It was.''

"I'm glad you found me." And Dirk was surprised to find that he meant it. "I won't do anything like that again.''

"Can we sleep now?" Tilden lay back on his bedroll. "I did some hard riding to catch you—it feels like my ass is stuck to my neck.''

Dirk smiled and sipped coffee and watched the boy go to sleep and thought how odd it was that life could flop the way it did. One day he couldn't wait to be rid of the kid, and the next day he was glad to have him back.

Then he closed his eyes and let the fire take him down.

C·H·A·P·T·E·R

☆ ─── *16* ─── ☆

D IRK opened his eyes and was awake instantly. He had gone to sleep with the Colt next to his head and he found it in his hand automatically.

He did not know what had awakened him and he lay with his eyes open trying to see in the pitch-dark of the new moon. The fire had gone down to nothing and there was no light. He heard Tilden's even breathing across the fire, and the rumble of the horses' stomachs from where they were picketed.

Then he heard it.

A small metallic sound. A scrape on a rock. The nail in a boot heel rubbing stone, or maybe the edge of a post spur sliding off a rock—somebody was moving out by the horses.

He eased out of his bedroll and worked barefoot down along the creek bed where they were camped toward the horses.

There.

A form, then another—two men. They were by the mule that had laid back its ears but remained silent, and Dirk worked until he was not more than five feet from them in the darkness. He could see no features but at this distance couldn't miss.

"Stop," he said. "Right where you are. Put your hands in back of your necks."

At that moment it could have gone either way. For part of a second the two men froze.

Then it was too late. They moved apart and Dirk felt the concussion of a handgun going off almost before he saw the flash from the cylinder.

In the sudden glare he saw two men, the horses and mule jerking, and then he fired. He aimed at the center on the first man and fired twice as fast as he could, sweeping the form down and away.

The second man meanwhile fired at him again and he sensed-heard the bullet go past his face as he thumbed the hammer and fired twice more at the remaining form.

It, too, went down and there was sudden, deep silence punctuated by a yell from Tilden who was up but confused.

"What's going on?" Tilden had his rifle up but

could see nothing and did not know really what had awakened him.

Dirk said nothing. He'd moved to the side and crouched during the firing and he now moved again to the side. He did not know if both men were out of commission, or if there were more, and he held the Colt in the direction of the two forms on the ground.

There was a short pain sound from one of the horses and it sagged and went down. One of Dirk's shots had taken it in the lungs, by the sound of it, and it died wheezing and still he held.

Waited.

Tilden yelled again. "What's happening?"

Neither of them moved even then and Dirk moved toward the men. He felt their necks and found no pulse in either of them and stood. Still waiting. If there was another man . . .

But there was not.

"Bring a match," he said quietly to Tilden. "I'm over here."

Tilden brought a handful of matches and Dirk lit one.

Both men were dead. One was hit in the middle of the chest and the other in the neck. He didn't know either one of them and wondered for a moment if they were part of the four men they were after—the two he hadn't seen yet.

"I know them," Tilden said.

"You do?"

"Not by name. But they work—worked for Parker. One of them helped lock me in the back room. I caught him good in the eggs—I'm surprised he could ride."

Again, Dirk thought, he seemed cool and calm about the bodies, but his voice had a tension to it—like wire stretched taut.

"They must have followed me," Tilden said. "Looking for you."

Well, that Bible-thumping son of a bitch, Dirk thought—no wonder he gave me the goods so easily. He always figured on getting them back. He was probably going to send these two after me anyway, and when the kid got loose they just followed him, hoping he'd lead the way. He dug in the pockets of the two men, felt a couple of coins, and put them in his own pocket. There was nothing else.

"Let's go," he said. He blew a second match out and made his way back to where the bedrolls were. It was still dark but the eastern sky was starting to show light and he knew by the time they made their rolls and saddled the animals it would be light enough to ride. "We got to get to Taos and get this over with—seems like all we've done is stack bodies and I'm sick of it."

"Ain't we going to bury them?"

"No," Dirk said. "We aren't."

"Oh."

Dirk rolled his blanket and slicker up. He

wanted a hot cup of coffee, but he wanted away from the dead men more than he wanted to take time to make a fire and sit and wait for it to heat. He poured some cold coffee in a cup and drank half of it down, swished another mouthful around and spat it out.

"Jesus," Tilden said, watching him, "how can you do that?"

"You swear too much."

"I'll swear as much as I like."

Dirk said nothing more but saddled the mule. Already the sky was light enough to make features out around them and Tilden hurried the catch up to him as he swung the twin sack-packs over the Indian pony and rode out of the gully.

He'd only come a day, a long day, but just a day, and what had Parker said—a week to two weeks to Taos? Even if the son of a bitch had been lying it couldn't be that far.

The mule and horses were in good shape and his ass was hardened off. He could push them, and the boy was tough as well. There was no reason they couldn't make it in six more days and get this dirty business over with.

He heeled the mule and set up a hard, pushing trot. As before they would do ten and ten. Maybe they could catch the bastards before Taos.

C·H·A·P·T·E·R

☆ —————— *17* —————— ☆

T AOS was the prettiest place he'd ever
seen.

Maybe it was the way they came on it,
just in the evening. They had ridden over Laveta
Pass and down to a small settlement named Fort
Garland, where some dusty soldiers told them
they had not seen the men or woman and then
pretty much ignored them. Then they turned
south and had ridden hard for two more days past
small settlements without seeing anybody but
Mexican farmers and peaceful Pueblo Indians,
south along a range of mountains that one old
farmer told him were named the Sangre de
Christo Mountains.

"The blood of Christ mountains," he had explained in broken English. "For their color, don't you see?"

And the next dawn they had emerged red, blood red with streaks that went out like veins into the sky, and they had ridden in that red beauty, pushing the mounts, until, finally, they saw the Taos Pueblo, where the Indians still lived and had lived—according to the same farmer who had told them about the mountains—forever and ever. Since the mighty mountain—the Taos Mountain—had first come from the earth.

Dirk had no idea about the truth of it, but the way the Taos Pueblo looked when they rode past it in the late-afternoon sun it could have been true. Something about it, the curved shapes of the adobe walls stacked on top of one another, the dusty rich color of the dirt—something about it looked incredibly old. As old as the earth. Tilden felt it as well.

"I ain't never even thought of anything that pretty," he said. "It makes you want to whisper, don't it?"

And Dirk had nodded without speaking, watching the Indians working in the cornfields next to the pueblo as they rode past.

The town of Taos was another couple of miles after the Pueblo and they came there in the evening, the western setting sun bathing the town in gold so that it—as with the Pueblo—was almost too beautiful to believe. Like a church.

I could stay here, Dirk thought. Live here. When this other thing is done I could just stay here and wake up in the morning and look at that mountain.

The mountain, Taos Mountain, towered over the small adobe settlement. There was early snow on the peak and the air was so clear it seemed to Dirk he could almost reach it.

The town itself seemed to have grown from the earth—the adobe buildings rising in soft lines and gentle curves.

Tilden had not said a word as they rode into town past an adobe hotel and into the plaza where cottonwoods provided cool shade; though the air was now cool enough.

Dirk thought the boy's silence was due to the sights, but when he turned he saw the boy was almost humming with tension. His eyes were wide open, darting from one figure to the next in the plaza, his hands tight on the full-barrel rifle.

In the center of the plaza some Indians in blankets sat, bent over, talking together quietly, and Dirk nodded to them as they rode past, but they looked up without answering the nod.

On the south side of the plaza there was a small saloon called La Cantina and Dirk decided to start there.

He dismounted and tied the mule to the hitching rail and left the boy outside.

Inside it was dim and he moved quickly to the side so as not to make a target of himself.

Which made him feel silly once his eyes became accustomed to the darkness and he saw there was only one other customer in the place—a drunk sitting at the back at a table brushing imaginary spiders off his arm.

The bartender, a fat Mexican man with curved shoulders like a bear, raised his eyebrows at Dirk but said nothing.

"Beer," Dirk said.

The bartender nodded and put a jar of warm beer on the bar.

Dirk took a sip. "Do you speak English?"

"Enough to get you a beer," the bartender answered. He sat on a high stool in back of the bar. "Which you have not paid for."

"I'm looking for some men," Dirk said. He took one of the coins he had taken from the two men Parker had sent—it proved to be a gold double eagle—out of his pocket and put it on the bar. "There will be three or four of them, possibly with a young woman with red hair."

The bartender shrugged and made change and said nothing.

Dirk took a long pull of the beer, swallowed it, and put the jar back on the wooden top of the bar. "One of them would be named Shaver, another Carley. . . ."

Another shrug.

Dirk went back outside.

"Anything?" Tilden asked. He looked out of place. A ragamuffin with clothes weathered and torn, his face burnt black by sun and fire smoke.

"Nothing."

They spent the rest of the short evening scouring the town, asking anybody and everybody and came up with nothing.

Finally, just before dark, they went up a small creek that ran east of town out of the mountains and made camp.

"They ain't here," Tilden said. "They didn't come here."

Dirk put beans in a pot and shoved the pot into the coals. The ham was long gone and he had forgotten to buy food in town with the change from the bar. Or anything. And there didn't seem to be anything to hunt—the Indians and Spanish had been taking game for hundreds of years.

"I've been thinking about it," Dirk said. "I think we must have passed them without knowing it."

Tilden waited, rubbing evening dew off his rifle with a piece of rag greasy with ham fat.

"If they left the fort and went over Laveta, they're coming here. There must have been a thousand side canyons and if they stopped in one of them we could have ridden right by and not seen them."

Tilden still waited.

"I have a plan," Dirk said. "We'll make another pass through town tomorrow, then head out north and lay up and see if we can catch them. Now let's try to get some sleep."

In the morning they broke camp after coffee and rode back down into town. A slight frost had come in the night and the mule was full of it, prancing and kicking and snorting, and Dirk had to fight to keep control of him as they came into the plaza.

Tilden was directly in back of him, pulling the pack pony, which had begun to dislike the mule and was working better in back of Tilden's Indian pony, and they came riding under the cottonwoods where the sleepy town was just awakening.

Dirk was looking down at the mule—which was crow-hopping sideways—and he looked up to see the man who had shot him in the face standing with a man he did not recognize by the hitch rail holding his bay horse.

It was too fast.

Everything was too fast.

"It's him!" Tilden yelled from the rear, but it was all too fast.

Dirk's hand moved toward the butt of the Colt but seemed caught in molasses.

He saw the man's face—a moment of puzzlement, then recognition and amazement—but the man was faster than Dirk and his hand was already on his gun, the gun coming up before Dirk's, the hammer going back, all so fast.

Too fast.

There was an explosion, the same white flash Dirk had seen before when the man—Carley—had shot him in the head. He felt the bullet slam into his left side and knock him sideways in the saddle so that he had to hold the horn to keep from going over and he thought suddenly how he seemed to be spending way too much time being shot by this son of a bitch and then the whole world turned upside down.

The mule was skittish around gunfire anyway and when the handgun went off in his face he left the plaza like an antelope, taking the nearest available exit—which was the narrow slot between La Cantina and the next building.

Dirk did not know how bad he was hit. There was not pain from the wound yet, but a stunned confusion—the beginning of wound-shock—and all he knew was to hang on to the mule. He had never gotten his gun out, was hit with it still in the holster, and he dropped it and grabbed the horn with both hands and stayed with the mule through a series of narrow alleys, over small fences and low walls, past smoking adobe ovens, and scattering chickens and children until he was suddenly out in the desert, the mule still pounding wide open.

Now the pain took him, came up from the

wound in waves. He fought it down and sawed the mule around and was surprised to see Tilden and the packhorse right in back of him, although the pack was torn apart and most of their gear gone.

"I . . ." He wasn't sure what he was going to say. Something about being sorry, something about going back and taking Carley, but it didn't come out. Just "I . . ." and he rolled to the side and went off the mule like a sack full of wheat and could think or say nothing. His eyes swam and he was gone.

The last thing he saw was Tilden scrambling down from his horse and kneeling next to him and then there was only a settling haze.

C·H·A·P·T·E·R

☆ —— *18* —— ☆

H E was not confused when his eyes opened, not totally confused. He remembered who he was and there was no doubt at all that he had been shot in the side. From the top of his ribs to his hips on the right side it felt as if he were on fire and he had to grind his jaws to keep from screaming with it.

He had no idea where he was, except that it was dark and cool.

He smacked his lips. They were dry and felt glued together. Tilden was there and he leaned over with a clay jug of water and put it to Dirk's mouth. He drank greedily, went too far, threw up—which played hell with his side—then drank a bit more and held it down.

"Easy, easy. . . ." Tilden spoke as if he were speaking to a dog or horse. "Easy, easy. . . ."

Dirk lay back. Some kind of bed, he thought, in a small room. "Where are we?"

"In a house," Tilden said. "Belonging to a Mr. Romero. He's kind of the law here."

"Kind of?"

"Well, he doesn't have a gun or anything. He's real old and knows a lot and just settles things. A whole bunch of women and kids came after us for running through their places and when they saw you were shot they carried you here and I just followed."

"How long have we been here?"

"I think about an hour. Old lady Romero came in and lifted your shirt and washed you and put some kind of grease on you and a thick bandage. Mr. Romero said it wasn't bad, just cut across the side."

"God. It feels like I've been cut in half."

"Well. That's what Mr. Romero said."

"What happened to Carley?"

"They took off. That other man with him was one of the men who . . . you know, was at my place. I guess they ran scared. I don't know. When your mule cut out the Indian ponies followed and I couldn't stop them. I tried swinging my rifle around to get a shot but by then we were between the buildings and I had all I could do to stay on, let alone shoot. That was some ride."

While he spoke he was standing and going toward the small door that apparently led to the other parts of the house.

"Where are you going?" Dirk asked.

Tilden stopped at the door. "These people said they'll keep you. I've got to find them and get Ellie back. I've already waited too long."

"You can't go alone."

"You can't ride."

Dirk said nothing. Instead he rolled sideways and to a sitting position. The pain was a roar up his side, but he controlled it. The tightness of the bandage contained the wound and he took short breaths. No ribs were broken. He was still dressed and he stood slowly. "Where's my gun?"

"They took it off you," Tilden said. "Hell, you can't ride."

"I can ride," Dirk said quickly, but he wasn't sure he could. "Do you know where they went?"

Tilden shook his head. "Not really, but old man Romero said Carley rode off to the north and there's a place out there named Seco, Arroyo Seco." The Spanish words came hard off his tongue, bent in the wrong places. "We came by it on the way down. He said there's water there and that's probably where they stopped."

"They must have come in right in back of us," Dirk said. "I remember the stream there, and the buildings." He tried three times to buckle his gun on before he caught the buckle. It was difficult to move his left arm without causing more pain than he could stand. "Lead out."

Tilden nodded and left the room ahead of him and Dirk followed. They came into a larger room with windows and a big table in the middle. An old man and woman sat at the table and Tilden stopped by them.

"These are the Romeros," he said. "I told them all about what we're doing."

They both nodded to Dirk but said nothing. Dirk thanked them for helping him. "I'm sorry about this," he said, "how we came into your house."

Still they said nothing and Dirk made for the door. Tilden was already outside. Just at the door, with his hand on the metal latch, he heard a cough.

"The woman with them, the boy's sister," the old lady said. "If she lives, bring her here. She will need help. . . ."

Dirk turned. She was sitting very still with both hands in front of her on the table, lying palm-down. The old man was looking at her and he nodded. "Yes. If she lives, she must come here." He looked up at Dirk. "I would help. There are others here who would help, I think, but I do not have a horse and cannot ride anyway because of my back. It is an old back. And it would take too long to get others."

"Bring the woman here," the old woman repeated.

"If she lives," Dirk said and left.

Outside Tilden had the mule ready for him and he used his right hand and arm to pull himself up. Once in the saddle he had to hold a second and regain control, then it wasn't as bad as he thought it would be and he kneed the mule into movement.

They went through town and out the road to the north, past the pueblo again. It was midmorning, cool still from the frost of the night, and the mule and horses were fresh and wanted to move and he let the mule out into a gallop. The trot they'd used through town was hard on his side, but the easy canter proved to be less of a problem and they made for Arroyo Seco on the winding desert road in good speed.

Dirk tried to plan but his brain could find no handles. He did not know what they'd find, or even if they'd find them again. They might have kept running.

Or not. Four men, all with rough edges, used to being rough—Carley probably thought he'd killed Dirk. Or at least put him down. Why would they ride away? There was no real law and they probably wouldn't worry too much about the boy, one boy, coming after them.

If he remembered right it was about ten miles

to the small settlement. The mule was moving roughly ten miles an hour.

When three quarters of an hour had passed with the mule loping easily Dirk eased off and let it catch its breath, pulled it down to a walk:

"What are you doing?" Tilden came up in back of him. The pack pony had slowed him, though not much. "Why are we stopping?"

"I've been doing everything wrong," Dirk said. "I'm going to try to do something right. We're close to Arroyo Seco. Before we get there we're going to leave the trail and go off to the side and see what we can see. . . ."

He stopped as he saw a side trail. "There."

The mule saw it and took it with a little knee pressure. It wound through sand hills and rocks but Dirk kept the mountains on his right and in a mile and a half they broke out onto a small ridge.

Arroyo Seco lay below them and he pulled the mule quickly back from the top of the ridge. He had seen nothing but had not had much time to look.

He dismounted—with some effort, his side was settling into a steady soreness now—and motioned Tilden to do the same. They tied the animals to some pinion trees and made their way on foot back up to the top of the ridge and studied the small canyon below.

Perhaps a hundred yards beneath them, down

a shallow incline, there were four dusty adobe buildings, huddled next to a muddy stream. Dirk and Tilden had ridden through it two days before on their way to Taos but had not stopped because they wanted to get to Taos as soon as possible.

The four buildings made up a settlement that had probably been there for two hundred years without changing.

There was nothing to see except the buildings. No movement. Not even chickens. And no horses tied in front of the buildings or held in the small rail pen that seemed to lean against the back of one of the smaller buildings.

"They're not here," Tilden said. They were lying on the ridge and he fidgeted with his rifle and made to get up.

"Wait." Dirk held him down. The army, he thought—always the army and the war came back. Wait. Hold and wait. Things happen if you hold and wait. "They might be there."

"Hell, there ain't nothing down there. . . ."

"Wait. And be quiet."

Tilden settled back. They waited.

A full minute passed, then another, and then Dirk heard it.

Metal on metal. A clinking sound. Not from the buildings but away to the right, farther up the stream that flowed from the mountains through the small town.

"I heard something. . . ." Tilden said.

"I heard it too. Be quiet."

Suddenly, quite clearly, Dirk heard a woman's voice swear in English.

"God damn you, leave me alone."

The voice cut up through the willows and piñon brush and Tilden's ears perked like a collie.

"That's her," he said. "That's Ellie. . . ."

And before Dirk could stop him he was up and running forward, over the edge of the ridge and down into the small valley.

"Wait," Dirk hissed, but it was too late. He was gone in the piñon and willow, the rifle held out in front of him. "Damn."

He held for a minute. The kid was going to blow it, he thought—running into four men. They had to be camped up the stream a bit from the buildings for some reason. Damn, damn, damn. . . .

His brain chewed at it. He could follow the kid in and they'd both be put down. Had to be fast, had to think fast.

The kid was running. He'd tear into them.

That was it. He could come in from the other side on the mule and let Tilden act as a diversion. It might work. Might. But it had to be fast now. . . .

He swung on the mule, ignoring the lance of pain that tore into his left side. The .45-70 was still tied to the saddle horn and he untied it, heeling the mule off to the right and over the ridge as he did so. One shot with it, then the Colt. Every shot had to work. Come in fast and get off the mule and get the gun working.

And it almost worked.

The mule did as he expected, as he wanted. It ran down the hill and to the right in great leaps, showering rock and sand, and exploded out through some thick piñon into a clearing that contained a small lean-to of adobe, open on one side, and the stream cutting through the middle.

Quick pictures, like frozen paintings.

The men by a fire. Two of them, standing. Horses tied on a picket between two trees, but sad-dled and getting ready to go. Another man and a woman with tangled, dirty red hair and a filthy, torn dress near the pickets. The woman thin and young, with one hand raised to strike at the man who was holding her with his other hand. A fourth man—Carley—halfway between the fire and the horses.

All staring at him, stunned.

And Tilden nowhere to be seen.

Damn, Dirk thought. The kid had held back. He rolled off the mule while it was still running, hit the ground hard, and felt something tear in his side but could not stop for it.

They had guns out now. Jesus, he thought, four men with guns.

The woman's eyes were wide, her mouth

opened in an **O**. Pretty mouth, he thought. Too bad.

And then it all happened at once. He raised on a knee and held the rifle on one of the men by the fire who was aiming at him, and fired, saw the big slug take the man down, and dropped the rifle and clawed the Colt out, fell to the right.

Everybody was shooting at him. He felt the snaps of bullets around him, saw dirt tearing, and he fired four times as fast as he could at the second man by the fire and saw him go down as well and had time to think, Good. Two. That was two.

Then it all went to hell. Carley and the man holding Ellie both fired and one of them took him in the leg he was kneeling on and he went over.

Can't, he thought. Can't go all the way down. He raised on an elbow and cocked the Colt, but it seemed to take a year, two years for the hammer to come back. Another hit, this time in his arm, and he was driven back and on his side. Damn. God damn.

He held the Colt up in front of him like a shield. All that was left, all he had, the gun. The girl had thrown herself away from the man holding her and was on the ground and Dirk fired at him, aimed at his chest and fired twice and saw the second bullet take him in the face and thought, Well, three. I did three of the bastards anyway.

And the Colt was empty and there was still Carley.

Another hit. Across his left shoulder. The Colt flew away on wings, whirled away, and he would die now. He knew that.

There was Carley, smiling, looking down at him.

Like before. His revolver aimed at Dirk's face again. The same. There would be the flash and then nothing. He'd done that before. It wasn't so bad.

"You die hard, you son of a bitch," Carley said. "But you *will* die. . . ."

Carley held stiff arm, held on his forehead and aimed carefully, and that would be it, but Dirk didn't care now because it was over, all over. He was hit hard anyway, hit and down. Everything was done.

Then an explosion, an enormous thudding bellow of an explosion and there was no flash, no end. Instead the center of Carley's chest blew out in a red spray, a giant red misty flower, and he was driven forward and down as if hit by a train; forward and down to drop in front of Dirk's face, the eyes already glazing with death.

And a last picture, the last thing he thought he would ever see.

Ellie sitting on the ground, her mouth still an O of surprise at all the bodies around her, and Tilden, short Tilden with the floppy hat, calmly and coolly reloading the sniper rifle, sliding the ramrod down into the barrel while he watched Carley die.

And then nothing.

E·P·I·L·O·G·U·E

NOT quite dead.

That's the first thing he thought when he could think. I must be not quite dead.

Before that his mind swam in muddy circles of pain and light and dark and he didn't know anything, didn't understand anything. Just murk and death and the awful, roaring pain that never ended.

And then the thought.

Not quite dead.

He opened his eyes finally, after what seemed days of thinking the thought over and over in disbelief, he opened his eyes and saw that he was in the back room of the Romeros' again, the dark room, except now there were candles everywhere. Stuck in small bowls. Candles all around the room on shelves and on a table and on the floor, small votive candles like yellow jewels shimmering in the dark room.

He couldn't talk but she saw his eyes open.

Ellie.

She was sitting next to the bed in a hard wooden chair and she saw his eyes open and she leaned forward.

"Easy," she said. "Be easy."

He closed his eyes and opened them again. Such a soft voice and the curve of her cheek in the yellow light was gentle and kind.

Then Tilden. Standing suddenly in back of her. "Mrs. Romero did things to you, put things in the bullet holes, and fed you with a hollow tube . . ."

Oh, he thought, yes, bullet holes. All those hits. He remembered them now, refelt the jolts. Jesus.

". . . until I thought you couldn't hold more. Ellie and me helped her. And Mr. Romero, too. We've been here two weeks."

All that light, he thought, still silent. Dark and light and dark and light. Those must have been days. Days and nights and days. Two weeks—two weeks dead.

"We killed them all," Tilden said. "Every one. And Mrs. Romero said if you made it through the wound fever you'd be all right."

Then he must have had alarm in his eyes because Ellie reached a hand to his forehead and pushed hair away from his eyes softly, gently, and nodded and smiled. "Yes. You're going to be all right."

He looked at her eyes and thought, Yes, I believe you, believe it will be all right, and he closed his eyes and let the soft rest come.